CHIMERA AND THE CAT BURGLAR

A FUC ACADEMY STORY

CYNDI FARIA

AUTHOR NOTE

Thank you to Eve Langlais for creating a zany FUC world I'm in love with. Also, thank you, Reader, for spending time with Willy and Boo on their quest to a HEA... as well as kicking some slithering Sssssnake ass!

I promise to deliver swoon-worthy monsters with every story.

Love, hugs, and happy reading,

Cyndi

ACKNOWLEDGMENTS

Edited by Devin Govaere
Cover by Rebecca Poole with Dreams2Media

ONE

Willy Tagger had never been more hissed off in his life. Okay, he was being dramatic, but as he strutted across the Furry United Coalition Newbie Academy's auditorium floor, he knew he didn't deserve his dedicated seat on the right side of the front row. It was within arm's reach of Boo Bombay, the sexiest feline shifter he'd ever laid eyes on, who just happened to be the high-school sweetheart that he'd ghosted.

It had been a dick move. Now, she wouldn't look at him, and he deserved that. But her ramrod spine and the object she was clicking inside her pocket proved her irritation and let him know she'd spotted him.

He swiped a bead of sweat from his brow.

He was her hated ex, her nemesis, and the one person she'd claw apart if she could. At least, he'd imagined how much she loathed him a hundred times.

He jiggled his leg to the tempo of "Back to December," which he sang in his head, remembering when he and Boo were a couple, a past that he'd ruined and one he shouldn't be focusing on. His Academy graduation hinged on him passing Forensics 101, in which he currently held a D on a good day.

He squirmed against his restrictive seat. No matter how he tried, this close to Boo, he couldn't peel his gaze away from her mocha glow while thinking about what she'd been up to these past four years. Her cat-shaped, lime-colored eyes tempted him to stare. Even if she wouldn't acknowledge him with much more than a subtle turn of her head.

She'd matured, rounded curves replacing the sleek angles of her youth. For certain, she was beautiful before, but now, even more so in his eyes.

Did he smell vanilla, bergamot, and jasmine perfume?

His heart squeezed though he pushed any rising feelings down. A relationship like the one that had been stolen from them was as moot as dead, fallen leaves and pruned apples returning to skeletal trees.

Still, he took in every nuance of her body. The cat shifter wore a Marty McFly jean jacket over a leopard print dress, the material shimmering from the overhead lighting. She'd cinched her hair into a neat bun, and he trailed his gaze down the length of her body. Her black ankle boots gave her a kick-ass appearance and did all sorts of twisted things to Willy's otherwise nonchalant facade.

Doomed. Yep, she was distracting to the point of failing the after-discussion quiz.

Luckily, Willy had escaped bumping into Boo over the past four years, and he cursed his acute scenting abilities, which homed in on her lip-licking pheromones.

The microphone squealed, pulling Willy out of his reverie.

"Welcome, cadets. We'll get started as soon as Agent Zeb Earhart arrives." Llama shifter Alyce Cooper, the

director of the Furry United Coalition Newbie Academy—
FUCN'A for short—stood at the podium, rapping manicured nails on the microphone's neck.

She wore a lavender skirt and a white top, highlighting
her ebony skin. Her updo and immaculate edges framed her
face. Her intense gaze highlighted the intelligence Alyce
was known for.

Willy held the highest regard for his mentor and sat
taller.

Boo shifted in her seat, and the air stirring from the
overhead register blew her scent in his direction a second
time.

He steeled himself as a wave of heat plunged through
his belly and set up shop in his dual dicks. Damn. He didn't
want to allow his experimented-upon body to shift and
expose his desire for the woman he'd never stopped
thirsting for, even in his dreams. Not that he'd let that
embarrassing thing happen. He could control himself.

He crossed his left ankle over his right thigh, proving to
himself that he'd mastered his abilities, including
preventing his body from succumbing to the effect Boo had
on his body and, if he was honest, his heart.

Ba boom ba boom ba boom. His heart ached, and he
wished he could turn back time, return to that senior year
in high school when he'd fallen in love and thought he and
Boo would be together forever.

It was a pipe dream now.

Loving Boo was a once-in-a-lifetime feeling, which he'd
tossed aside to become a FUC agent. That was before the
jailed mad scientist DIC—Dr. Icabod Crick—had
kidnapped and experimented on him. Now he needed to
pass Forensics 101, and then he'd charge into his future as
an international FUC agent. He'd get out of town as soon as

he endured this symposium that had zip to do with his class.

Life was always throwing obstacles in the way of his dreams, which was why Willy wore running shoes and was fit enough for hurdles.

"Please welcome FUC Agent Zeb Earhart." Alyce clapped.

The crowd mimicked her excitement and welcome, including Willy, who slapped his palms together a few beats.

If Alyce gave an order, Willy wasn't about to challenge the llama shifter. She'd been responsible for saving his life once upon a time. Also, a FUC agent rarely shared an artifact before delivering it to its museum of origin, in this case, the Grand Egyptian Museum.

Willy could only hope to turn his interest in historical finds of the furry kind into reality. He was, after all, a history buff, spurred on by movie characters like Indiana Jones and Nathan Drake.

"If you'll all take your seats, we'll get started." The only unruly thing about the impeccably dressed agent was the mass of waves on top of his head. He placed the cloaked item on a raised pedestal and hovered his hand over the scarlet velvet cover.

Willy studied what lay hidden beneath the cloak. It was two feet tall and cylindrical. He tasted the musty sands of forgotten caverns, shivered from the chill of underground tombs, and felt the heart-thudding excitement of finding an artifact like the one sitting center stage.

As an experimented-on gorilla shifter—colloquially called a Lump, although Willy preferred chimera—he had heightened senses similar to felines, like detecting movement in low light, an acute sense of hearing and smell, and a sense of touch enhanced by long whiskers that protruded from his face and other places when he shifted. It all allowed him to hunt effectively at dawn and dusk.

Those attributes could have brought him further in his forensics class if he'd been allowed by the instructor to use his abilities instead of adhering to required forensic facts. *"There are other courses that allow you to embrace your animal side,"* the instructor had said. *"But in this one, we're focusing on good old-fashioned brainpower only."*

The agent wasn't a chimera, but the shifter did possess acute hunting abilities.

Will crossed his arms and extended his legs, placing one ankle over the other. This show-n-tell was all right. His forensic class was the toughest of them all, and a break from the class, or rather from stressing about passing the class, was what he needed to brighten his outlook.

He couldn't deny that Boo certainly took his mind off the stress.

Failing wasn't an option, and he wouldn't accept it.

Not after he'd failed Boo.

She wouldn't even look at him.

Boo was on the edge of her seat, leaning inward, now fiddling with the stone on the necklace that hung around her neck and focusing on the presentation instead of him.

He wished he was as focused.

The agent adjusted the microphone and removed the cover from the object.

The blinding violet aura surrounding the item forced Willy to shield his eyes, but that didn't stop them from tearing up. It also didn't keep his skin from popping up quarter-inch gooseflesh, most likely some genetic attribute DIC had plucked from an avian shifter and injected into his new DNA.

Something was happening to him.

Fuckin' A.

Willy glanced behind him to the audience. He scented the air, searching for the acrid scent of adrenaline wafting from the other cadets. He turned his ears, listening for increased breathing.

Not a single newbie seemed to be affected like he was.

Well, except for Boo. She grabbed her neck and started hacking as if she were going to yack out a hairball front-row center.

His protectiveness over her sparked, sending an electrical jolt down his spine to his phantom tail. Willy scooted closer to the cadet separating them, nudged the nose-twitching capybara shifter to trade places STAT, and took up his new perch next to his ex. "Do you need water? What can I do to help?"

As if Boo had seen a ghost, her round emerald eyes lit up, and she swallowed hard, looking at him. "I'm okay, and not your problem."

Willy fought his expression from twisting up at her rejection as she jumped up and headed toward the next row behind him.

He kicked himself for believing she'd want him to be near her or help her. She hated him, and he deserved her ire. Despite knowing this, he still couldn't help but feel her revulsion also had something to do with the monster he'd become. Sure, he was in full human form now, but everyone knew what he looked like shifted. Although he'd accepted how his gorilla looks had morphed to become more tigerish, he was sure not everyone had.

Luckily for him, his drive to protect Boo didn't send him into a tailspin. He remained seated, but he watched her out of the corner of his eye as she grabbed a free seat not too far from him.

She's fine, he reminded himself. She'd survived without him for four years, and she'd be okay after he was long gone, when his dreams of becoming a FUC agent took him to faraway places.

He hung his head briefly before forcing himself to focus on the display.

Zeb tapped on the microphone, testing it before starting the presentation, a wide grin displaying the man's pride when he held up the artifact.

From where Willy sat, the artifact resembled a golden phallus. However, focusing on the object through the nearly blinding aura, he could make out the legless elongated torso and the dome-headed feline.

"I located the statue inside an Egyptian cavern, and it's believed to represent the goddess Bastet from the third millennium B.C. It contains feline properties of wisdom, intelligence, and independence, as noted by the intricate hieroglyph carvings." Zeb pointed to the engraving that marched up and down the exterior.

Willy noticed a heart-shaped divot under the cat's chin, like something was missing.

Boo raised her hand toward the ceiling. "Is it true that anyone without feline ancestry is cursed after touching the item? Is that why you're wearing what I suspect are leaded gloves?"

Willy narrowed his gaze at Boo, a memory of her teen years rising. Her family owned the Willow Wisp Museum. They specialized in feline artifacts, so it didn't surprise him that she'd know unique details he didn't.

His lip curved upward, and his pulse kicked up.

"I'm wearing gloves to protect the item and can't verify

if it's magical or cursed." He glanced around the room, adding a chuckle before continuing. "However, it is rumored that Bastet was the goddess of wet dreams."

What was with this agent? His comment was lewd, but most agents seemed charmed by him. Worse? Boo seemed captivated by the man who was not only buff but also—if Willy was honest—as good-looking as James Bond and any of the actors who'd played him in the movies.

The crowd's murmurs turned to giggles just as the overhead lights went dark.

Willy blinked, his eyes adjusting quickly to darkness. He could make out the agent standing beside the glowing Bastet artifact. But as the agent stood, waiting for the lights to come back on, the artifact floated.

What was happening?

The traveling violet aura surrounding the moving statue caught Willy off guard. He realized someone was stealing the artifact. He moved without thinking, without saying anything. His voice lay trapped behind his lips, but his feet were already on the ground, chasing after the suspected thief, who threw open the exit door and bolted into the night.

Willy was close behind the thief. The sound of stealthy footsteps disappeared around the exterior corner of the auditorium. Before Willy could decide whether or not to shift, his body exploded out of his clothes, tiger-like pads landing on the solid concrete walk that snaked around the campus. He paid no mind to his insignificant nymph wings, but he used his puma tail to balance as he gave chase.

The speed of the culprit took Willy by surprise as they skirted the Academy lake at the fringe of the campus. As a Lump, he could transform his head, and he did so now, allowing him to speak. "Stop, thief! Stop now!"

The shadowy figure put even more distance between them.

Willy yowled as he scented the air, inhaling the powerful fragrance of feline pheromones, which had mixed with the sour taste of adrenaline flooding his veins. He realized the statue could be dripping with an intoxicating, mind-controlling scent that had him licking his lips.

The dim lighting from an overhead lamp post cast a brief glow on the figure he chased as they rounded the lake, and the thief disappeared into the row of academy housing.

Close... Willy was so close that gooseflesh blanketed his skin, but he couldn't identify the robber.

Dodging and weaving, Willy made his way down the row of houses. When he popped out to the other side, coming upon a grassy quad, he thought he'd been given the slip until he spotted depressions in the grass, which he suspected were footprints.

Willy dug his claws against the spongy surface, finding purchase just as a sinister shape darted into his view. The chimera leveraged his hind legs and propelled himself into the air. The thief was within reach.

Willy would be labeled the hero of the day. He would pass his class or, at least, earn credit for recognizing the faintest of clues and his quick-thinking heroic actions, which all FUC agents shared.

He sank his pads into rounded shoulders, and the two tumbled onto the sloped portion of the Academy landscaping. He ignored the familiarity of the womanly figure under him. How her furry curves melted against his when they rolled, her landing on top of him and then the two trading places as they continued down to the bottom of the slope. How he'd missed connecting with another feline shifter, something he hadn't realized he needed until now.

He retracted the nails that pinned the culprit under him when they came to rest where another walkway met the lawn.

"I've got you, thief! There's no escaping Willy Tagger."

"What in the rats' hell, Willy? Get off me. Get off me now!"

Boo?

The moment Boo's strong yet sweet voice reached his ears, his face heated from embarrassment, and he sat back on his haunches. He held his paws in the air, surrendered to his novice mistake, and quickly transformed into his human form. "I'm sorry. I swear I thought you were the shifter who stole the artifact."

"Me? I was tracking the thief. I'd have him if you hadn't gotten in my way." Her big round eyes took in his partial nudity—the shredded clothes he wore hanging on but covering nearly nothing—pausing on his maleness. "How did you even know it was being stolen?"

He covered himself. Although nudity was a shifter thing, Willy felt, well, vulnerable in Boo's presence. DIC had changed him in more ways than physical. "When the lights went out, I saw the artifact being lifted and moved."

"How?"

"I saw the purple aura."

"That's impossible," she breathed. "Only a feline shifter can see it."

"I'm no longer a gorilla shifter, as you saw. I'm a chimera. I'm more feline-based, more like the big cats, but that may change. Which is why I noted a thief with feline attributes making off with the artifact."

Boo huffed and smoothed her hair. "Well, you're not wrong about the thief being feline, and it's not surprising. The artifact leaks feline scents like toxic catnip. It's irresistible to cats and cat shifters, but it has other qualities, which, in the wrong hands, could be deadly."

Willy considered her words. "Well, what other feline shifters were in the FUCN'A auditorium? If we've deduced that the thief is feline, then I'd guess the agents have already figured that out, too. All eyes could be on the two of us for stealing the artifact, but I whiffed a smelly cat, so obviously there were at least three—me, you, and the thief."

Boo hissed as she glanced around the nightscape, a lamp illuminating the quad in gray tones. "We're key witnesses, but I can't get involved, and you know why. If anyone finds out about my past, I'll get expelled, possibly sent to prison. I'll never prove to my mother that I'm more than a gravedigger."

He nodded grimly. Willy had promised Boo he'd protect his knowledge of her teenage past, and that would never change. "Your secrets are safe with me."

A flashlight beam roamed over the duo before landing on Boo's face. Agent Earhart—Zeb—stood over them, a hand balled at his side, his chest pumping from running, his sharp gaze demanding answers as he asked, "What secrets?"

TWO

"None of your business," Boo replied, batting at the white beam of light Zeb directed at her eyes, the ray reaching the back of her guilty brain.

"You'd better check that attitude," Zeb snapped. "I know a thief when I see one."

Boo swallowed hard. He wouldn't be as easy to convince as Willy had been. Could the agent see all the rule-bending things she regretted in her past that led to her family disowning her? If so, she was heading back to jail before she earned her family's forgiveness by delivering the Bastet heirloom back to where it belonged with her family.

If only someone hadn't made off with it during the assembly, thwarting her own plan to steal it.

However, she didn't have time to debate whether stealing the artifact would have led to redemption or damnation. She needed to throw Willy and Zeb a bone and dig herself out of this hair-balled, failed plan to steal the statue.

She glanced away and threw up a defensive hand. "Get that light out of my eyes, Agent Earhart. Like, seriously, you're wasting time here when you should be hunting the real thief."

The agent took a step backward and dropped his hand, the glow of the flashlight illuminating the space where she and Willy had left an imprint on the grass.

Clear as the night, she recognized the outline left on the sod of their entwined limbs and her ass cheeks. Embarrassment flooded her fiery cheeks, and a tickle started in her throat. The smudge on the grass looked terrible, like they'd been sneaking out and doing the nasty, comparable to when they'd lived under their parents' roofs.

She coughed until her head spun from lack of oxygen. At least she blamed her swimming mind on that, not on Willy rubbing a small circle on her back and telling her to breathe. It was the first time he'd touched her in four years.

Could my night get any worse?

Trying to defend what was left of her honor—not that she had much left with a rap sheet the size of the Great Lakes—she said, "This isn't what it looks like."

Really. Believe me.

"Don't tell me what to think, cadet." Zeb jabbed his index finger her way. "I know this wasn't a little tryst out here. I heard the two of you talking. What's this secret you're bent on keeping?"

"It was nothing." Yet it was everything. Would Willy be true to his word and not reveal it? She didn't want her past shared with some agent who could be a quick judger like her mother, Cecilia. Crap. Maybe Boo should have worked the hanky-panky angle. It would have been better to let the agent think that than deal with the third degree.

But Boo's feline intuition told her she wasn't getting out of this situation quickly.

The bone. Throw the bone, Boo. But what could she say?

A chilly draft shot up Boo's backside, proving how vulnerable she'd let herself become, and she slapped down the hem of her dress. It was a stupid move to think she'd absorbed investigative experience by being *near* FUC agents.

She felt exposed. Dang it. "Let meow explain."

Zeb raised his palm, silencing her, and turned the beam on Willy, giving him a raised brow at seeing their intimate proximity. "What were the two of you doing out here?"

Willy readjusted his shredded shirt, so it covered his two swinging privates. Those were new. *Well, at least one of them*, Boo mused. There was much she didn't know about her first love now that he was a chimera.

"I'll take it from here, Boo."

Her heart squeezed at Willy's attempt to protect her morality.

Willy cleared his throat. "I saw the artifact floating and its lavender aura hanging midair when the lights went out, and I chased after the person taking it."

"You saw a purple aura?" The agent rubbed his chin. "You're a Lump... er, a Chimera."

"I'm an experimental survivor. My new DNA is seventy percent feline. And apparently, anyone who carries a feline gene would be able to see the aura."

The agent narrowed his gaze as if he hadn't known this tidbit.

What else didn't he know? Boo had been surprised when he'd been unable to answer questions about the artifact earlier, and this further proved that he knew nothing. Strange. He didn't appear incompetent. He was a FUC agent and a badass, but not everyone knew everything the world had to offer, including ancient artifacts of the feline variety.

"Is that your story, too, Cadet Bombay?" Zeb thrust his chin in her direction.

Boo flicked her phantom tail, her heart pounding in her chest. Zeb seemed to believe Willy, but that was because he was the trustworthy sort. Boo never had been. And while she might not have been the one who stole the artifact, she'd sure intended to try.

Would her lies cover up the fact that she'd wanted to seize on an opportunity to clear her name with her mother and her entire family? Bringing the artifact home was her shot at proving everything she'd done previously had been to benefit her family long-term. It was returning the artifact to its true owner and not some thirsty, no-name museum where it could fall into the wrong hands.

Intent alone was enough guilt on her conscience to make her look suspicious.

She cleared the rising hairball from her throat. "Willy's spot-on with his detail. We both saw the item floating when the room blackened because we are feline shifters and detect the object's aura."

"Willy's not a purebred," Zeb corrected, his expression as stiff as a scratching post.

"You're splitting hairs. I saw what I saw," Willy said.

Her pulse sped up. She was excited by Willy's defense, turning around her irritation at how things had gone down between them. "But big cats are his new genetic strength. So, he may have been born a gorilla shifter, but he's clearly strong in feline attributes now like he mentioned, including agility and intelligence."

"That's true." Willy beamed.

She stood taller, resisting an eye roll. She'd mentally discarded arrogance, neuroticism, and impulsiveness.

Would she have hesitated to chase after the thief and

the artifact if she'd thought Willy would stand between her and her goal? If she could have known that he'd get her dragged into an investigation? She wasn't prepared to solve the case of the missing artifact—especially considering that if she found the thief, she'd take the artifact for herself—but she could tell Willy was ready to prove his skills.

Battle of the egos much?

Boo sighed. She had an idea for the cocky agent. "I don't think anything more needs explaining, Agent Earhart, regarding our reasoning. We're FUCN'A cadets. It's in our blood to protect the furry kind."

"But they managed to evade you?" Zeb lifted a brow.

Boo winced. "Unfortunately, yes. If only we had your *keen* eye and *savvy* investigative skills, perhaps we would have had better luck."

The agent lengthened his spine, appearing taller. "Which is why I'm asking both of you to come with me. Director Cooper will want to know exactly what you saw as key witnesses before I cut you loose."

"Key witnesses?" she yowled. "I didn't see enough to be of any help. The one who took the item is probably a mile from campus now, and it would be a better use of your time tracking him instead of questioning us."

Willy shoved back his shoulders upon standing. "Or he could be hiding in the classrooms, dormitory, hell, the cafeteria where they keep the meatless meatballs. I chased him around the back forty and through the dorm buildings until he gave me the slip. I thought Boo was the thief, but clearly, she's not hiding a two-foot cat-headed phallus under her skirt."

The two roamed their gazes over her, as if she could conceal the artifact under her dress.

Scratch my eyes out now. She pulled her jacket and dress to reveal her silhouette. "I don't have it."

On me... Yet.

"Let's see if we can't backtrack." The agent motioned for the duo to follow him and raised his cell phone to his lips, updating his team.

She dusted herself off and plucked a blade of grass from her hair, sampling the fescue between her teeth. She couldn't help sucking as much folic acid out of the culm section of the plant as possible.

This was the start of a long game of the chimera and the cat burglar, and she needed all the nutrients she could get to boost her O2.

"I lost him here." Willy thrust his hand, the one with the crooked pinky finger, toward the block wall dividing the one-story classrooms from the three-story dorms.

Willy was digging them a hole, one Boo had no business lying in. She wanted the artifact, but she also wanted away from the authorities. The only way she'd be able to take the artifact for herself was if she was on her own and not being babysat by Agent Earhart.

"Now, hold on." She raised her hand and crowded the space between Willy and Zeb. "Let's not get too big for our britches. I'm sure the agent can find the thief on his own, considering they were too slippery for cadets like us, no matter how heroic we thought we'd be."

"Too heroic? Is that a thing?" Willy asked. "I want in. That wily tomcat was feral and undomesticated. A true threat to society. I plan to help find him and see him locked away."

Locked away? Boo shivered and choked back a hiss, remembering her own time in lockup. She thrust her hand into her pocket, gripping her blade, the one she'd found so long ago. It provided comfort, and she could use all she could get.

"With what evidence?" The agent pinned Willy with a hard stare.

Willy tapped his nose and sniffed. "I may be unable to identify the culprit's physical specifics, but I know stink when I smell it. I can't get that rotten egg stench out of my sinuses."

Both the agent and Willy wrinkled their noses.

But in truth, his words worried Boo. The person who stole the item wasn't the true threat; the artifact was. It was the object that needed to be locked away where it would never be found... It just so happened that specific place was inside her family's museum vault.

As much as she wanted to get away from the agent, she had to admit that any help finding the artifact was useful. "Yes, yes. I believe Willy's right. This fella needs to be rooted out, and sniffing him out might work. I think we should start with a sweep of the academic buildings."

"Follow me but keep back." Zeb sprinted toward the classrooms, his leather loafers slapping against the sidewalk and his black jacket giving him the illusion of wings.

That man was as much of a beast as Willy, both men extraordinary fit.

But it was Willy her heart pined for, dang it.

Willy motioned for her to go ahead of him, and he took up the rear, both jogging after Zeb.

Her stomach knotted, and she could only hope they wouldn't be barraged with more questions as they came upon a swarm of fresh agents.

"Spread out," Zeb ordered. "These two cadets chased the culprit. They believe he entered one of the classrooms. But be warned. The suspect may be a skunk shifter."

The agents skittered outward, leaving Willy and her standing alone. It made her think about the object, how some believed it had magical properties to turn back time.

She didn't know if rewinding time was a good thing when it came to Willy and her. What would it be like to be back in a time when they were in love, back before she'd been jailed?

He'd been carefree; they'd both been picturing a future that no longer existed.

Her mother had still showed signs of loving her.

Boo shook her head, willing the thoughts to go away. She would not cry over her loss. In life, there were no true re-dos.

Willy surprised her by asking, "So, do you really believe the artifact is cursed?"

She blinked, surprised at the question. "How do you know that?"

"You had asked Agent Earhart about it earlier, in the assembly."

Right. She'd wanted to get a feel for how much Zeb had known. She shrugged, playing it off. "All I know is that some say the object is so mesmerizing that it will call for you to touch it, and when you do, you'll no longer be of this time."

"Of this time?" Willy's leaned in. "Are you saying some actually believe it's a time travel device?"

Boo pumped her shoulders. "I've only heard stories, but they're bad, Willy. No matter how the statue beckons to you, promise me you won't touch it."

Willy's brows knitted together as if he wrestled with his options. "The agent did."

"He was wearing leaded gloves. Those gloves kept him safe, but I'm not sure if the agent understands the severity of the curse, should he slip up." She lifted her hand, realizing she was stroking an unfamiliar arm.

Willy was no longer the boy she once knew. He was a *man*, muscular in all the right places, secure in his new form.

And here she was still stuck in the past and trying to make amends with a parent who no longer called her on her birthday.

Willy sidestepped, putting a good foot between them. "Why are you suddenly worried about what I'm doing or what happens to me? I know I broke it off after I was kidnapped and dealing with shit. I get that you'd hate me for that, but when I got better, I called you and you never returned my calls. You didn't care when I needed you most, so don't bother now."

She opened her mouth to question his logic, but the reality was she had resented him because, even though he'd suffered, he seemed to embrace his new life.

While she'd allowed her bitterness to keep her in the past.

She'd put distance between them after he broke off their relationship. She'd been in her own world then. She hadn't gone to see him. She hadn't returned his calls. She'd been angry at the world, jailed for a time, and then unsheltered before Alyce Cooper found her and offered her an opportunity to find her place in this furry world.

Boo hadn't found it yet.

If she'd stayed with Willy, she'd have only screwed up his future. Maybe she already had, even though she'd never stopped thinking about him and caring. "I never want to be the cause of your pain."

"Same..." Willy shuffled his feet and kicked at the marbled walkway between the row of classrooms.

A shout echoing from one of the classrooms pierced the night.

Birds chittered above the treetops, and boots clamored toward the call for help.

Boo put up fists and took a defensive stance, fine whiskers popping out on her face and testing the thickening tension riding the air. "Something's happened to Zeb."

Willy was already jogging toward the crush of agents who raced toward the location.

Boo had a choice. She could follow... Or she could run in the opposite direction and use this distraction to go off on her own and track down the thief.

Her legs stiffened. Something disastrous had happened, and she had no business getting further involved. Yet...

"Hey, I need you." Willy waved her onward. "Boo, come on. Now is our chance to make a difference, to help, and for our elders to see us as more than underlings."

She looked across her shoulder, meeting Willy's determined gaze.

"Running away from problems is your go-to. How are you my daughter?"

Boo's mother's accusations threatened to send Boo into a haunting spiral.

But as Boo stared at Willy, a dizzying wave rolled over her, and his words looped two more times as if time was waiting for her to make a spectacular choice.

"Hey, I need you." Willy waved her onward. *"Boo, come on. Now is our chance to make a difference, to help, and for our elders to see us as more than underlings."*

Was it dèjà vu? Had someone touched the item and rewound time to this moment? Why did she feel a pull, like fate was telling her to face her fears? To make amends? That Willy could be her future?

She didn't believe any of it, but her feet seemed to have a mind of their own, leading her toward Willy, leading her toward the agent in trouble.

Boo squeezed through the mob of black, wool suits, snagging her silken dress as she followed Willy into the building and down the hall, entering a classroom and spotting Zeb.

Zeb lay on his back, holding out his hand, reaching for her through the swarm of agents. His blue eyes welled with tears. "The Chosen One."

Who? Boo glanced behind her, only spotting Willy in the classroom. Certainly, neither of them was special.

Zeb curled his fingers, summoning Boo. "Come closer..."

She bent down, lining up her ear with his lips, listening to Zeb.

"Thirty degrees, 34 minutes, 22 seconds, N, 31 degrees, 30 minutes, 36 seconds E, June twenty-second," he uttered, and then he disappeared.

What was significant about those latitudinal and longitudinal coordinates? And that date?

But mostly, Boo wondered, *where* had Zeb gone?

THREE

Gone! Zeb had vanished.

Willy continued staring at the empty space where Zeb had lain inside the classroom, Boo by his side.

Willy blinked, not believing his own eyes, but when Boo looked up with shock on her face, he knew she'd seen the same thing.

Boo's earlier words about a curse rang in his memory. Had Zeb come into the classroom, located the artifact, touched it with bare hands, and then fallen to its curse?

Ridiculous... curses didn't exist. Objects weren't actually magical.

But that empty spot where Zeb had just been made Willy question everything he once thought true.

Then the air shimmered in iridescent hues. Boo's gaze ripped from Willy's, and they both stared at the spot where Zeb had been, just in time for the faintest image of Zeb to reappear, darkening until...

Holy guacamole, Zeb returned!

But where had he gone? Willy hadn't the foggiest idea, but he crouched, assessing the agent.

Zeb's limbs remained slack, and the man's ashen complexion gave him a deathly look, but Willy could just make out the slight rise and fall of his chest. Zeb's eyes were set in a half-opened position. Zeb might not be dead, but he seemed to be frozen in some kind of limbo state after reappearing.

"Willy, do something." Boo blinked up at him, demanding help.

Willy's throat knotted with emotions, making it impossible for him to give voice to his racing thoughts of awe, fear, and dread. But he pushed through his pain, calling out, "Medic. We need a medic."

"Move back. Everyone, give the man space."

The stagnant commotion behind Willy seemed far off, but he recognized Alyce's commanding presence as she came to stand beside him.

She pressed a phone to her ear as she phoned the medical team, gave directions, and then clicked to end the call.

She knelt beside Willy. "What happened, and why is Zeb unconscious? What's going on with my agent and cadets?"

The alarm in her tone spun Willy to face his mentor. Alyce asked the question everybody wasn't asking while he was trying to convince his mind that Zeb *had* disappeared before reappearing and he had witnessed the impossible.

Willy swallowed repeatedly, trying to rid his throat of emotion so he could answer Alyce. It hurt his heart to see the unconscious agent's limp hand in Boo's and her wiping tears with her free hand.

Feeling the weight of the situation pressing down on him, he responded, "I believe Zeb came in contact with the statue when he found the thief hiding in the classroom and fell victim to the curse."

"Curse?" Alyce placed a hand on the passed-out man, feeling his pulse along his neck, and then opening his eyelids and inspecting the dilated pupils.

"Will he be okay?" Boo asked, her voice cracking.

"He's no more cursed than any of us," Alyce said with a shake of her head. "I suspect he's been poisoned, and as for the rest of you? Smells like a lot of cannabis."

She looked at the agents who'd straggled in behind her, some who appeared about ready to pass out, others with goofy grins on their faces.

Willy recalled the skunky scent from earlier. He was no expert, but he was pretty sure the scent came from animal pheromones, not a plant product. He didn't like doubting Alyce, but in this case, he was pretty sure she was wrong.

"No. Time suspended." Willy murmured, trying to make sense of his experience. "Poison doesn't make people disappear."

"What Alyce is saying would make sense," Boo told him softly. "The statue is said to be cursed, but folklore often has a scientific explanation. Perhaps in the case of the artifact, it has to do with toxins that are released and cause hallucinations."

"That's not what I witnessed." Willy leaned into the conversation, unwilling to give into Boo's argument. "The agent actually vanished for a full five seconds."

"I know it *seemed* that way, but it was an illusion, from the *toxic fumes*." Boo narrowed her gaze and coughed into the crook of her arm.

Was Boo warning him not to interrupt her again? Willy said, "Go on."

"I'm uncertain how far-reaching its mind-bending

attributes extend," Boo admitted. "It's probably dissipated enough that it's not affecting you, Director Cooper, and it's not affecting me and Willy as bad as some of your agents because we're feline shifters. It looks like Zeb got the worst of it because he probably had physical contact with the object."

"Your theory seems sound." Alyce nodded. "We need all agents looking for this thief before some unsuspecting person falls victim to it like Zeb did."

Willy grew rigid, his shadow under the light elongating. Not only did he object to being talked over, but why was Boo lying to Alyce? Boo wasn't mentioning the time distortion, how reality seemed to hover in the air, freezing everyone except for them. He was looking at Boo the entire time, and there was no way she hadn't seen the same he had.

This meant there had to be a good reason why Boo didn't want Alyce to know what had happened, and he planned to get to the bottom of it as soon as they had a private moment.

For now, he kept that to himself, considering the side eye Boo shot him, which he'd seen a time or two in the past. Not all information needed blasting, like what DIC had done to him.

Or why Boo had been charged as a grave robber.

Willy shoved revisiting that nightmare behind him. What did the pain he'd endured or the fact that Boo had been charged with desecration of a corpse have to do with their current problem?

Nothing.

Their skeletons were better left in the past. Shame had caused both of them to change and twist truths.

He set his focus on making sure no one else got hurt.

Willy gestured toward the open window behind him that led to the outside quad. In the distance, he could make out the cadet housing, and he noticed the full moon descending. "We're wasting hours standing around. There could be another afflicted by this paralyzing toxin if they get trapped with the object like Zeb."

Alyce threw up her hand. "Whoa, whoa. Have you forgotten that you're still cadets? Under my protection here at the Academy? You're not full FUC agents ready to go out on a mission to catch a thief."

Willy glanced outside the open door. Several agents were sitting under the moonlight, their heads hanging between their knees, as if that time distortion had affected them physically and they were still trying to grasp reality.

Alyce touched Willy's arm to get his attention.

She motioned to the open window inside the classroom. "What you can do to help is give me all the information you have on the situation. Did either of you see the suspect?"

The window was the first thing Willy had noticed and his ability to recognize an animal's heat signature proved the thief had escaped using that window, the heat dissipating as he stood there watching the lavender aura fade.

"No," Willy said. "We never saw anyone leave the room once we found Zeb. Thankfully, Boo and I are unharmed."

Alyce sighed. "Thank goodness."

Willy rolled his tight shoulders, begging the knots to unravel. The very thought of something terrible happening to Boo threatened a migraine to explode behind his eyeballs.

But the fact that he and Boo were unaffected was his bargaining chip. "If feline shifters are less affected than non-felines, wouldn't you want to use all of them you have to track this thing?"

Alyce retrieved her cell phone. "I'll call in feline agents from other offices."

"And they'll be here a day late," Willy retorted. "While we're here, now."

Alyce clucked. "Like I said, I'm not comfortable getting you two involved."

Meanwhile, the burglar was getting away. "But I am. I'm ready now."

"No." Alyce jabbed a finger in his direction, making sure he understood that she called the shots when it came to her cadets.

"Then let me do it," Boo piped up. "I'll track down the thief so no one else will get hurt. Zeb needs medical attention, and while he's getting the help he needs, I'm your best choice."

"You?" Willy scoffed. "I'm a chimera with superb healing abilities. I'll go." The faint sound of agents approaching alerted him to the medical unit's arrival at the open door.

"Neither of you are going." Alyce helped Boo to stand as they allowed the medics to tend to Zeb.

Once outside, Alyce said, "I won't send any cadet without a backup. We're not going to charge into this without a plan. I need time to gather some feline agents and brief them."

That didn't sit well with Willy. Knowing the object was out there and could affect the unaware worried Willy. Any unsuspecting person could be in close proximity and fall ill, like the agents had. Letting time pass without acting to retrieve it seemed a poor decision.

Willy urged, "Alyce, call in all the feline FUC agents.

Brief them. Get them up to speed. Let them join Boo and me when they're ready. But let us get started now so the case doesn't stagnate."

Alyce let out a deep breath. "Fine, this is what we're going to do. I will get started bringing in agents, but the two of you aren't going to go off half-cocked. I don't have time to interrogate you on anything you witnessed, seeing as I need to organize a feline team. So I want the two of you to start working on this case by going into town, getting some food, and getting down all the details you can, so I can add it to the mission brief."

Willy smiled, surprised yet pleased that Alyce finally relented. "Thank you."

"You won't regret it," Boo added.

"I better not." Alyce watched the medics wheel the ashen-skinned agent out of the classroom on a gurney.

A medic stopped to tell Alyce, "We can't know if Zeb touched the object before entering the auditorium or if he came in contact with the poison inside the classroom."

"Or if we're all part of a time-bending matrix," Willy muttered under his breath.

Willy no sooner made that comment that Boo picked her head up and shot him a wide-eyed warning glare.

Buy why? Why did Boo demand his silence?

"Hallucinations is what Willy's referencing," Boo said.

The medic nodded. "The poison could be monkshood, cyanide, arsenic, ricin... Both the sweet scent of chloro-methane and the rotten-egg smell of hydrogen sulfide were picked up in the classroom. The symptoms were similar to ingesting magic mushrooms or peyote or licking cane toads."

Willy had met a cane toad shifter. The thought of getting the man's ooze on him caused Willy to shiver.

Or did he shiver from fear and from the idea of someone using poison to keep a person from directly handling the artifact?

He broke off from the two women and followed the gurney, stopping after a bit to watch them wheel Zeb off to the medical wing.

Boo came up behind him. "Zeb looks bad, and it's my fault."

"It's no more your fault than it is mine." Willy defended his ex. Boo had always put others before herself. Even in grave robbing, she'd had the best intentions.

He recalled all the details about Zeb he'd observed with his acute chimera sensory capabilities. "Zeb didn't have tremors. He wasn't drooling. His heart wasn't pounding outside his chest. He may have been poisoned and fallen victim to its effects, but something else is wonky with this missing golden wanker, and that has nothing to do with you. Maybe Zeb had an enemy targeting him specifically."

Boo inched closer, brushing her arm against his as she shook her head. "The statue's designer could have applied poison to deter the wrong person from using the statue maliciously, but if someone wanted Zeb dead, he'd be dead."

"And Zeb is alive. He's heading to the med wing where they'll figure out how to revive him. He's in the best hands, and it's up to the best felines, who happen to be the two of us, to solve this case."

"You mean we happen to be the only felines at Alyce's disposal," Boo countered.

"Which makes us the best." Willy winked then glanced over Boo's head, noting that Alyce gave them space, turning to her agents and speaking to each.

Alyce caught Willy looking at her and lifted her index

finger, showing him she wasn't finished with them yet and not to leave.

Boo took the free time to corral Willy. "I was serious when I said you should stay away from this. Whatever the cause of Zeb's condition, it's serious."

"Really?" Willy asked incredulously. "Look, we don't have time to debate this. Alyce doesn't have a feline shifter at her ready. It's up to you and me to find this phallus and bury it where the sun doesn't shine."

"I'm not working with you on this." She shook her head and took a step away from him.

"Why?" Memories of the bad blood between them surfaced. "You can't let the past between us stand in the way of us finding a dangerous artifact. As FUC cadets, we're sworn to protect—"

"It's not that," she interrupted. "It's not about my feelings for you. It's about the fact that this artifact is dangerous, more dangerous than you know."

"I don't understand why you're being so strange about this. I have feline DNA, just like you. What makes you better suited for this than me?"

She bit her lip before sighing and admitting, "The truth is the Bastet statue is part of my lineage and belongs to my ancestors. I'm the only one who knows how to handle it safely. A man is unconscious. I don't know when or if he'll wake up, and I don't want you chasing after something you have zero knowledge of, trusting or targeting the wrong person, and ending up like Zeb."

He heard the truth and real worry in her voice. While Willy never backed down when he made up his mind, Boo had him questioning his intention.

Willy recalled his past. He'd made the mistake of not being careful once, and it had been the worst mistake of his life. He'd kept quiet about the strange feeling he had about a man following him around their hometown of Willow Wisp when he was eighteen. He'd trusted the man because Mr. Duke was a local bus driver who'd driven Willy home from elementary school and beyond with his Bernedoodle riding shotgun. So when Mr. Duke asked for help looking for his lost dog, Willy had entered Mr. Duke's van without a second thought.

Then Mr. Duke, aka DIC, the mad scientist, used Willy's easy-going personality to his advantage. DIC had jabbed him full of poison and inflicted Willy with scientific shit he still didn't understand and couldn't explain, but it had permanently changed him.

Missteps could be deadly or life-altering.

But Willy wasn't going to take his past as a lesson in hiding and playing it safe. He signed up for FUC training because he wanted to be a hero. He wanted to protect others from danger.

Willy shoved up his sleeves. "I want to help find the person who did this to Zeb and return the artifact."

"That golden feline is deadly. Is that so hard for you to understand?" Boo let out a long exhale.

Maybe she cared about him still.

Nah. She was in it for herself, pushing him away, still trying to earn her mother's approval like she had all those years ago.

"We can't waste a minute talking about it. Just accept that we'd work best paired up since we're both immune to the artifact."

"Allegedly immune," Boo added, lowering her shoulders.

Willy asked, "What aren't you saying?"

"I don't want you to get hurt. Satisfied?" She shifted one foot, giving him her profile.

He visualized her flicking her long, curvy tail in defiance. Her confidence drove him wild. She was sexiest when she was sure of her limits, reminding Willy that he was still learning his new body and, along with it, his desires for a new future.

"Willy and Boo." Alyce tapped each of their shoulders as she came up behind them, trying to infuse her control over the frustration everyone was no doubt feeling. The director often showed how much she cared about her students, as if they were her children.

Alyce looked each up and down. "Instead of convening the feline contingent of FUC agents here, we're all going to fan out. If the item is dangerous, as it seems to be, the thief will want to unload it quickly, so we're going to head to different towns and investigate dealers, auctions, museums, and the like. Since you two are from Willow Wisp, I'm tasking you to go there."

"As in, on a mission?" Willy couldn't believe Alyce was actually assigning them to the case.

Willy gaped briefly before closing his mouth. Finding the artifact was his one chance to show he was ready to become a FUC agent.

Fly with that, Professor Condor.

"Thank you, Director Cooper." Willy beamed. "We won't let you down."

"Don't be rash, Cadet Tagger. The world is counting on us to locate that statue." Alyce pulled both into a private huddle. "I don't know what kind of poison boobytraps this artifact has put on it, and I don't take putting my cadets at risk lightly. Little is known about the stolen artifact, according to Mr. Ramet, curator of the Grand Egyptian Museum."

Apparently, Alyce had contacts.

"Legend says only Egyptian royalty—a lineage that sprang from an Abyssinian shifter—can destroy the artifact's power."

"What's an Abyssinian?" Willy asked.

"It's an ancient breed of cat," Boo explained. "A lean and stealthy feline with a smooth, ticked tabby coat. Each individual hair is banded in different earthy colors, making the cat appear orangish."

Willy thought his fur resembled that, although he'd come to label himself more of a puma shifter than a tiger when his chimerism sent him in a feline direction when he shifted.

Then Willy remembered something. "Zeb mentioned a Chosen One before he fell unconscious, but I'm no more an Abys shifter than Boo, so if it's not us, who is it?"

A thought flashed through his mind that DIC may have injected him with some ancient breed... He wouldn't put it past the jailed mad scientist.

"Tagger, we know better than to believe folklore that talks about curses and magic." Alyce shook her head. "Whatever Zeb said to you in those moments were the utterances of a sick man."

Boo cleared her throat. "So, we're to go to Willow Wisp and put out feelers for some black-market dealings?"

Just then Alyce's phone chimed. She looked at it, and a smile formed on her face. "And here is a good lead for you. Apparently, there is a black-market auction taking place there in three days."

Three days. A lot could happen in that amount of time. Waiting that long seemed like a waste of Willy's talents and abilities, but what else could he do? Search every corner of every town in the area? He might not like it, but Alyce's lead was the best they had.

"Won't it look weird, the two of us returning to our hometown together?" Boo asked, drawing him out of his thoughts. "We might not be able to get intel if we're walking around, looking suspicious."

"Good thoughts, Cadet Bombay," Alyce replied. She thought for a moment before declaring, "What would make the most sense is if you returned as a couple. Fiancé and fiancée."

"What?" Boo and Willy both screeched at the same time.

An engagement of convenience?

Alyce nodded confidently. "Yes, this will work. I'll get you tickets and a monetary allowance."

Boo gasped, and her eyes morphed into the size of quarters. "Now, Alyce—"

"It's the only way." Alyce snapped her jacket.

Willy's heart stuttered.

Boo had fought against partnering with Willy not five minutes ago. He doubted she'd go along with him as her sidekick, let alone his fiancée for this gig. But he'd take whatever punishment she dished out to help a future fellow agent, even if he had questions. "To what degree do we have to showcase our relationship?"

"Just be a convincing couple." Alyce twisted a ring on her finger, the diamond as large as an olive. The more she twisted and the further the ring slid to her fingertip, the surer the assignment became.

"I don't have to like it." Boo's gaze drifted as Alyce handed the ring to Willy.

Willy clutched the ring. Alyce fawned over her students,

making sure every detail fit the part. He held out his hand, asking Boo for hers, remembering when he'd dreamed of slipping a ring on her finger for real. "I don't bite."

She rolled her eyes.

Willy's chest tightened. She had loved when he'd nibble that spot below her ear, and she'd climaxed every time he'd taken her from behind and sank his teeth into her shoulder, claiming her.

Boo coughed, and he thought she might sputter up a hairball at the idea of their fake engagement, but she inhaled and placed her hand in his. "Fine."

He pushed the ring onto her manicured hand, the red polish highlighting the beauty of the stone. "It's fake, Boo."

Until I can make it real.

CHAPTER

FOUR

With the status of Zeb's medical condition unknown, Boo forced herself to take a seat to the right of Willy in the corner booth inside the local diner, the night darkening their cozy seating arrangement. She willed herself to accept they had to work together if they wanted results, which meant she needed to get comfortable with Willy to the point of passing off their fake engagement.

The overhead light illuminated his chiseled jawline and high cheekbones, giving him movie-star looks she hadn't noticed under the moonlight.

It was funny how life repeatedly switched things up. Willy threatened her best-laid plans of perpetual celibacy. Her body thrummed in his presence, despite her foiled plot to steal the artifact. "I know more about the ar-tion, er, I mean, artifact and auction and its players."

Did she stumble on her words?

She was doomed to fail in their mission if she didn't pull her scruff together. "Which is why I think it best that I lead."

Willy scoffed and set his coffee cup on the table, dark-roasted liquid rushing over the sides and pooling in the saucer. "Why? Alyce assigned us this together, presumably as partners. One not superior to the other, considering we're both cadets of the same level."

Fighting for leadership would foil her plans. She worked best alone, but if she was forced to work with a partner, she needed to be sure he wouldn't go off half-cocked. "We won't find anything if you go in there all cocky and willy-nilly."

"So that's your technical term for how you think I'll charge in?" Willy jiggled the table, his outstretched legs finding a rhythm against the table's legs.

He was hiding his frustration about as well as she was, her fingers tapping the edge of her plate. Boo had plotted every itsy-bitsy detail of her heist, and she hadn't been prepared for things to go so awry. She didn't want her assignment to go just as badly. "If you hadn't chased the original thief, Zeb wouldn't be where he is now, and we wouldn't have to pull off this PDA spectacle."

"I'm a spectacle?" Willy scoffed.

"You know what I mean," Boo countered. "This engagement farce is a spectacle."

"And you think I'm the reason Zeb is down? Do you think I forgot that *you* were out there chasing the thief too? Or are you saying that *you* would have caught them, while I would have failed?"

"You did mistake me for the thief and tackle me, which thwarted both of our efforts," she pointed out.

They stopped talking as the diner server placed Boo's veggie pot pie in front of her.

When she left, Willy continued, "You just keep negatively labeling me at every turn. But you're mistaken. You're mad at the wrong person. We're both running after the same thing, which means we'll achieve our goal of finding the statue faster if we work together without any power struggle."

Boo tried not to roll her eyes. The confines of the corner booth crushed in on her, but she willed her quickened breath and frayed nerves to calm. Willy gave her plenty of space by sitting on the adjacent side, nearest to the window while she sat against the solid wall as if the sturdiness became her spine.

He'd always been respectful at least, if also a bit reserved. And he was right. They both wanted the statue returned to its rightful owner. "I promised Alyce I'd stick to the plan, but I didn't expect she'd force us to pair up in this way."

Boo held up her ringed finger and tipped her body away from Willy. They were far from convincing anyone they were happily and blissfully engaged because she was fighting their union like an alley cat and a raccoon over pepperoni spoils behind a pizzeria.

She righted herself and dug into her steaming pot pie. "I don't like any part of this forced situation. I mean I don't know how to do this couple thing. I've always charged my own path."

Willy waited until the server set down his waffles and a tall stack of sizzling vegan bacon. The bacon was so crisp that it shattered when he cut through the stacks. The bits sprinkled his over-medium eggs, which sat atop his tall stack of waffles as ordered. Amber maple syrup dribbled down the side.

He chewed around his mouthful. "You've not always

been so singular. We made a good team once, and we'll find our way again. We'll fool everyone if we practice touching, hugging, making out, yada yada."

Yada, yada?

Boo was in the middle of drinking her iced latte, and she spat the beverage across the table.

Of course, Willy was right there, having jumped from his side of the booth. He stood over her, consoling her, dabbing at the corners of her mouth with his napkin and probably thinking she had a choking condition that required medical attention.

His suggestion to *practice* and his touch felt too intimate, hackles sprouting on her nape.

Boo had walled herself off entirely. The barrier encapsulating her heart had been impenetrable. Until now. Until Willy's tenderness attempted to break her. What would happen if she unleashed unresolved feelings centered around him?

She waved him off. "I'm fine. You can sit."

"You're nervous. As stressed as a mouse wrapped in sticky tape. We can return to Alyce and tell her we can't do this." He retook his seat and lifted his brows, waiting for her to answer.

His concern made her question her confidence. "I don't need coddling every ten seconds. I'm okay. I'm perfectly righty-ho with this assignment. Confident."

"Are you sure?" Willy reached for her arm.

She flinched and regretted her reaction. She wasn't the same person. Or rather, she was still angry at the world for punishing her for doing the right thing: returning her family heirlooms to their rightful owners.

If caught pilfering again, Boo was looking at a decades-long prison term.

She'd just have to not get caught.

She'd find the thief and take the artifact from them to return it to its rightful place. But to pull it off, she'd have to lean into the fake relationship... and allow Willy to touch more than her face and arms.

She sighed and admitted what was bothering her the most. "What if I screw this up? I going to cross paths with people from my past who recognize me, and I can't guarantee a smooth reaction."

Though she kept an apartment in her old town, she had managed to keep a low profile, spending most of her time at the Academy and most certainly never going near any of the underground auctions she once frequented.

"You're not the same rash girl you were in high school." Willy had returned to his seat, where he now jammed another forkful into his mouth.

She wished she was as sure. She wasn't rash enough to do anything without giving it serious thought after the blunder today. She had to be careful at the auction. She had to present as if she were high society instead of a convicted felon.

Willy was quiet. She expected some comeback, but perhaps they each had people they never expected to cross paths with again, in his case, the doctor who'd turned him into a chimera.

She was sure Willy was in the clear. Steel bars imprisoned DIC. He held no more significance in Willy's future.

Turning her thoughts to the task instead of the trail of shit she'd dragged with her to the Academy, she asked, "So this practice... What do you have in mind?"

He took a long swig of his coffee, wiped his mouth with another clean paper napkin, and set both aside. He extended his hand in her direction, palm up and his fingers beckoning Boo to take a chance. "How about we start with you not choking every time I touch you."

She flicked her eyes to Willy's. It was the first time she'd noticed that even his brown gaze held a depth it had lacked when they were dating. There was much she didn't know about Willy, the man, the chimera, the FUCN'A cadet acting as an agent. "You noticed?"

He stretched his hand toward her another inch, his one bent pinky failing to fully extend. "You're wound so tight I'm afraid we'll derail this mission before we start. Why don't we take a step in the right direction?"

Willy wasn't wrong about her tension. In a black-market auction like this one, they had to choreograph their moves like they'd been intimate for years, and not years ago, if they were to be invited to private events.

She analyzed his massive palm and thick fingers. *It's only a hand. It's harmless.*

Yet, tremors riddled her, keeping her from remembering how safe and secure Willy had once made her feel. It had taken her four long years to feel secure in her world, albeit without anyone watching her back, something she longed for.

Willy may have matured, his mutations making him bulkier than she remembered, but he was still Willy inside. He was still the man she'd crushed on so hard in high school and the man she'd thought she'd marry. Now, he was asking for her consent.

She took a breath, trapping it behind her lips, and placed her hand in his, taking a chance on them and their assignment. His skin was hot to the touch but dry. He ran a thumb over the top of her hand, drawing lazy circles over the peaks and valleys.

She felt confidence in those hands, and his fingers had once orchestrated her body to perfection. "You're warm."

"A cozy one-hundred-and-eight-degrees Fahrenheit." He closed her petite hand in his larger one and tugged her closer. "I know you find it hard to trust me, but I won't disappoint you. Promise."

No one could guarantee a future without disappointment.

Willy's warmth settled Boo's nerves, but she couldn't be sure if Willy would accept her if he found out she wanted to steal the statue for herself, but that was neither here nor there. She had to become comfortable with him so they could get close to the statue. What happened afterward...

She cracked her mind and heart open, adding a smile she realized hadn't blossomed fully since their breakup years ago. "So, what's our backstory?"

"I'm your partner," he said, releasing her hand to take a bite of food.

"That's a given. How did we meet?" She swirled the melting ice in her latte, mixing the milky concoction. She wondered if he'd make up a new story for them, or feel it best they went with their true origin, if he remembered it.

"We were high school sweethearts, of course. We met in biology on dissection day. You took one look at that limp toad and lost your cookies." He shoved a forkful of food into his mouth, and a dribble of egg landed on his lip, which he licked.

Boo had dug up shifters and human corpses. She'd seen everything, but that first time stuck in her mind. "It was horrible and the start to dissection reform. Students now have the option to deny participating in something so brutal."

Willy downed the last of his coffee. "So that's our origin story."

"Most of it. You helped me to the nurse's office and waited until my mom picked me up. Then, after school, you showed up at my house, telling me that the rest of the class had walked out and refused to torture that poor formaldehyde toad."

"That's right," Willy purred.

Boo smiled at the memory. "It was a heroic thing to do on your part."

"You were important to me. The problem occurred when I tossed every one of those soulless amphibians in the garbage and the students had nothing to dissect. Doing that earned me a weeklong suspension and a failed grade." Willy chuckled, and the table jiggled enough to slosh her watered-down latte.

The sound of his laughter strummed her own. She had been important to Willy in the past. However, tension had filled that time of their life.

It had returned. They'd survived turmoil once. Could they again?

She added to the memory. "Which the school board overturned once your parents lawyered up, and we celebrated—"

"With our first kiss at the park. It was perfect." His smile widened, and the table stopped jiggling.

Had their shared memories calmed him? She had yet to find peace. She spun the melting cubes in her cup. "That's not what I remember. It was windy. My hair kept blowing between our mouths."

"Nothing wrong with kissing hair to get to the good stuff." He pumped his brows.

The night they'd upped their intimacy tenfold on the

sands of Casper Beach, but she forced that memory into the deep recesses of her mind.

The pleasure he'd given her was something from the past. She needed to remember when they searched the auction for this new player that their engagement wasn't real. "I think that's enough backstory for one day."

"Not nearly enough." Willy hummed and inched closer. He roamed his gaze over her outfit, pausing at the thin gold belt that accentuated her figure before landing a look at the dangling loops swinging from her earlobes.

What was he doing? PDA now?

"You're still perfection. Still put together." He reached out his hand, taking the fine gold between his fingers. "You're not seeing anyone, are you?"

He dropped his hand, and she longed for warmth but settled on finishing her savory pot pie. Craving Willy was off the menu. She should be relishing the nutrition to help her think and collect herself.

She shoved a large bite into her mouth, the buttery sauce and dough bringing her no more pleasure than their fake relationship and the dangerous mission.

"Did you hear my question?" Willy leaned in, cutting the space between them in half and rounding the corner of the table to her side of the booth, his leg brushing hers. "I need to know if I'm going to piss off anyone when we kiss."

She dropped her fork, splashes of gravy splattering the table. "Kiss? You're moving too fast."

"Not fast enough if we're going to catch this crook." He moved closer, aligning his mouth with her ear. "Answer the question. Are you seeing anyone?"

"I'm not dating." She held back the fact that she hadn't been with another man since Willy.

Nor had she been familiar with black-market auctions since being taken into custody.

However, she could picture him kissing her as if it was yesterday. Her memory sent a fever to the pit of her belly.

She angled her body to face him on the bench seat. "You'll need a black tux, and I'll need a formal gown. These events are as much about who's who as they are about fooling everyone. We're only buyers representing a bigger player."

Willy leaned back against the cushion and narrowed his eyes as if not fully grasping their assignment. "Representing?"

Of course, they'd need to make up someone they'd be standing in for. "Oh yes, royals, politicians, the influential, and the wealthy."

With her successful pivot of the conversation, he retook his side of the table and tossed his handful of crumpled napkins onto his plate.

Those bigger players would see right through them if they didn't perfect their stories and PDA. "So where did you propose to me?"

She felt her shoulders relax, confident Willy could create a good one. Thankfully she didn't have to craft a wedding because someone might try to verify their marriage license.

"It was a beachside proposal without witnesses." Willy tore a fresh napkin, the edges resembling the incoming wavy surf. "I got down on one knee while you were staring at the horizon and picturing our future children and our family adventures."

"Oh really?" Boo considered the suggestion, her heart threatening to explode. She'd always wanted a beachside destination wedding, yet the proposal he'd described felt as magical.

Willy wrote their history as if he wasn't just spitting random details. He knew she was estranged from her mother.

She ventured to ask, "Which beach?"

He held up a finger, the wheels behind his brown eyes churning. "The mist wraps around the beach just enough to keep the onlookers on the bluff from gazing at the couple at Casper Beach."

A surge of memories stole her breath, and frankly, the reminder of how they'd once loved each other erased any sense of faking her feelings or their story.

Was he trying to get a rise out of her? Dissecting a past she'd buried? Trying to ignite a spark between them that she'd snuffed out years before?

She scooted to the edge of the seat and glared. "What are you doing? Why are you torturing me? Are you out for revenge because I ghosted you instead of the other way around?"

Willy huffed as if offended. "It's not my intention to hurt you. I'm only solidifying our backstory so we don't get outed at this first auction."

"Well, I don't want to remember, Willy," she yowled, capturing the attention of the single night-owl server. "I want to make a new narrative. One that's believable."

"What's better than the truth?" He held her stare and then spotted her twisting her fake engagement ring.

Nothing. Nothing was better than the first day she'd made love to Willy on that sandy beach, under the starlight, the waves orchestrating their intimate dance. But it was too real. Private. Whatever was happening between them turned as prickly as a sea urchin.

She punched to her feet, leaving Willy to settle the tab with the diner's overworked server.

How dare Willy stir up their past.

She marched off, wanting to hide her longing for a past that was no longer achievable.

Willy called out, "I'll meet you at ten in the morning at the Blue Flame Boutique in Willow Wisp for our first date, *kitten.*"

Could Willy set his mind to mastering his and Boo's first fake date, even though spending time with Boo was never pretending when it came to his heart?

Willy pulled curbside at the Blue Flame Boutique in Willow Wisp, his VW bus leaving a splash of smoky exhaust to hang in the misty air. He couldn't fix his bus now, but he would work to repair his strained relationship with Boo after last night's dining fiasco.

They needed to come together to catch the thief. Bickering be damned.

Boo stood beside the *Re-Elect Mayor Joystick* banner, outside the trendy fashion spot, her dark ringlet curls swishing about her shoulders. Her orange dress complemented her glowing skin tone, and her denim jacket matched her high-top Keds.

The boutique wasn't the only one whose fashion had improved over time.

Yowza. Willy's heart thudded as he took in the sight of Boo against the backdrop of the voguish storefront. He remembered the place, recalled the sheer, white gown that had once been on display in the window. Boo had shown it to him, telling him she dreamed of wearing it on their wedding day back when they'd dated.

Today, a lacy white bridal gown with a nude undertone draped the mannequin. Bows topped the shoulders and the ends fell softly down the back.

The dress was stunning, and Willy watched as Boo appreciated the design, a gentle smile playing on her lips. Was she wiping a tear?

He exited his van, shut and locked the door behind him, and then measured Boo's temperament as he approached her. Cortisol didn't have an odor, but an increased level stirred other bodily scents. Was she wearing rose oil to calm her nerves?

"Hey, you look nice. Casual suits you."

"Thank you. We have much work to do." She motioned to the window display, her smile turning upside down. "I hope what they have inside isn't as hideous as this year's wedding style, or we're wasting time."

He held up his hands, more in defense of her tone than her dislike of the dress. "Let's give it a chance."

He wasn't only speaking about the store, and he hoped she didn't make their date miserable, but something was wrong. He guessed, "Have you eaten? How about Wispy's Diner before shopping?"

She waved a hand. "I ate a handful of strawberries, you know, because of the antioxidants and vitamin Bs. Let's do this date."

The date wasn't a yoke on his shoulders even if she acted like it was to her. Experience hinted that the date wasn't the only thing bothering her. "You want to sit inside my bus and talk before we go inside? I know we left off last night on a curve."

She shook her head and motioned to his vehicle. "Not really. I'm surprised you're still driving that hippie-mobile. But it appears you don't break promises."

Willy had sworn the day he took possession of the van that he would never sell the bus since it belonged to his grandfather, who'd made him work all summer before he handed over the keys to the classic '70s van. Together, they'd worked hard to restore it, and that rig now contained Willy's blood, sweat, and tears.

The bus still wasn't perfect, but like his and Boo's relationship, it had been a work in progress. Now, a second chance presented itself. He would do better, be better, and prove to Boo he still loved her.

"I remember many things that happened inside, as well as a few unfulfilled promises."

"Don't spark any ideas." She jabbed her index finger his way. "This is a fake date, remember?"

It's real to me.

Never in a million years would he forget making love with the sexy feline. But he wasn't one to force their union.

She carried anger toward him because he'd yet to show her he'd changed since letting go of his anger over being experimented on.

Still, he gave her a way out. "Once we retain the artifact, we can go our own ways if that's what you want."

Boo strolled closer to the van and ran a hand across its polished fender, the ring catching the sun's rays. "The auction is two days away. That's all we're both obligated to attend."

Willy hardened a look. He had this lying thing down if she believed he'd forget her after this was over.

But was his facade enough to fool the thief?

He joined her at his van. "The exterior shell has seen

better days, but the custom peace sign painted on the back still defies muscle cars."

"That's true," Boo added, kicking at a stray weed embedded in the sidewalk near the white-rimmed tire. "Some things root deep and resist dying."

Take the inside of his bus. *And my feelings for Boo.*

The leather tuck-and-roll bench seats were the best versions— supple and welcoming. The front passenger bucket seat was open and ready for that special person to join him on adventures. Just like Willy's heart was waiting on Boo to slide inside and reclaim her spot beside him, both of them captaining their future, if she changed her mind about loving him.

He joked, "You need a refresher in the back before we head into the boutique?"

Boo spun to face him, her eyes going wide. "Don't think we're shagging. I'm on a mission. That's it. I'd no more crawl into the back of that thing with you than pretend—"

He waited for her to finish her comeback, and when she didn't, he finished her sentence for her, "Pretend we're engaged?"

"Yes, that's what I was going to say." She gave him her back and sashayed forward, her dress swishing musically about her knees as she reached the door to the boutique.

He met her at the door and grabbed the handle, keeping Boo from disappearing inside the store among the circle clothing racks. "This bitter banter is butchering my idea of a perfect fake date. If we don't warm up to each other, our success is doomed."

She blew a breath, dropped her hand from the door handle, and gazed up at him, water lining her lashes. "I'm not good at this do-over. I'm agitated, and it's showing. Maybe we should start fresh."

Huh? Did she mean it?

Willy's pulse amped up. "Listen, I know you're beating yourself up about what happened regarding Zeb and possibly in our shared pasts. None of this is solely your fault, no matter how much you think it is. Zeb didn't follow protocol, and he knew the risks. I just took off, making as much of a mess as you think you have. But we can turn this around if we leave our past behind and live in the now."

He waited for a beat, the sound of her rapid breaths slowing. When he thought she was calm, he held out his hand, offering to seal the deal. "Shake on it?"

She glanced toward the van, her eyes becoming unfocused as if she remembered all the good times they had inside.

He sure did.

She placed her hand in his, squeezing. "Deal. But remember, we're no longer love-blind teens. This game is about saving futures and lives."

And hearts.

Willy held the door open, allowing Boo to enter the store, her fragrant rose oil scent rushing up his nose.

That sense of calm was false, or at least, temporary. They had to bridge the awkward gap to deepen their romance because real life didn't make time for masking, and they had only one shot.

"Welcome to Blue Flame." The store employee breezed through the rounders that held a multitude of evening wear.

She wasn't much more than a teen herself. Freckles lined the bridge of her nose, giving her a look of innocence.

"I'm Fanny. Let me know if you need any help."

Willy stepped forward, inserting himself between the rounds to address Fanny. "We're looking for evening attire for a formal engagement tomorrow night. I'll need fitting for a black tux, and Boo needs a formal gown."

"Do you have a color preference?" Fanny asked.

Boo pulled Willy to the side. "Usually, I would prefer red, a power color."

Willy ran a finger along the silky fabric of a goldfinch-colored gown. Since he was a child, a rambunctious gorilla shifter, he'd found order and control in colors. Blues tended to calm him. Reds had him swinging from the chandeliers.

"Yellow represents hope, joy, inner freedom, and expectations for the future—something we're both trying to understand," he said. "Red fashions represent passion and love, and we're not there yet. Plus, I don't think standing out is what you want, right?"

Boo chirped a cool, "Mmm. I like the way you think. Yellow works for me."

They'd agreed on truth and honesty, even if Willy avoided vulnerability as much as Boo seemed to.

"How about these?" Fanny held up an assortment of sunny-colored dresses for Boo to try on. "Once you say yes to the dress, we can match it to the tuxedo's accessories like the tie, pocket square, cummerbund, vest, socks, etcetera. Follow me."

Willy trailed Boo, the sway of her backside sending him into a trance as if she were the magical artifact.

The salesperson hung the three dresses inside the dressing room. "If you need another size, yell."

"Give me a moment." Boo stepped into the curtained dressing room and closed the floral fabric wall.

Willy sat on a low-profile chair, which folded his knees toward his chest, giving him a fine view of Boo's adorable feet. Everything about her sent a zing of desire straight through his body. He wished he could turn back time—an impossible dream, which he parked. He couldn't allow himself to become distracted.

Stick to the date, a fake *date.* "How's it going with the first dress?"

Boo threw open the curtain. "Puff sleeves in a kaleido-scope of primary colors and a waist tie as long as the CanAm highway."

Willy cupped his hand over his laugh. The tropical colors would certainly gain attention or become the perfect camouflage. "It'd work for a toucan shifter."

"Which I'm not." She jerked the curtain closed, and a few moments later, it parted again. "Oh, now I'm a comb of plantains."

Punching to his feet, Willy couldn't hold back the laughter. The yellow dress gloved her curvy form from neck to ankles, and the sleeves and pattern caused his mouth to water. "Take it off before *I* get hangry."

Boo said, "I've almost forgotten you're a gorilla shifter among all the other animal genetics you carry. Let me try this last one. Fingers crossed it works."

Willy's angst jumped up. If they didn't find the perfect dress soon, they'd be in a bind. "Any luck?"

He crossed his fingers, even the crooked one, and all twelve toes.

"Well, the straps need taking up. And the slit up the leg isn't as high as I prefer." Material rustled, and then the curtain slid open, revealing Boo's gown. "I'd want the slit mid-thigh. That would look good, wouldn't it, Willy?"

His bottom jaw would have landed on the floor if the muscles and cartilage weren't holding the hinges together. Boo was having a full-on conversation with Fanny, but he noted only moving lips. What spell did Boo have on him?

"Well, say something, Willy, or is it another fail?" Boo batted green eyes at him.

The yellow was more mustard than sunshine, a shade darker than the deepest yellow sunflower.

Tapping his chin, Willy sought the perfect manner to describe the shade while returning to the present. "Spicy."

"Ooh, so you like it?" Boo's face glowed, a big white smile displaying pleasure at his meager feedback.

"Less is more." Willy whistled and then reached for her hand, spinning her around. The spaghetti straps needed taking up, and the mid-knee slit needed lengthening to make it easier for Boo to move in case they found themselves having to run. But what he saw caused a sloppy grin, and he nearly drooled. "You look amazing. Marigold is your color."

"I need shoes, but I can try on some while you're getting fitted." She kicked at the hem and then attempted to slide the curtain closed.

Willy gripped the cloth's edge, his heart ramming his ribcage and his feelings for Boo, real feelings, bristling. "Not so fast."

"What are you doing?" She slid her hand down, brushing her pinky finger with his.

He flicked his gaze to their flirting fingers as they both tested each other. "I think you know what I'm about to do, *kitten*."

"Kitten... You called me that last night. I thought you'd forgotten." She inched forward, the boned bodice of the dress pressing against his chest. "I thought you'd never call me by my nickname again. But I'm not naive, William. I know what's going to happen at the end of this. You'll leave on assignment, and I'll get my heart broken. There's no reason to believe anything between us has a real chance."

He stepped inside the room and closed the curtain behind him. He raised his hands, placing one on either side of Boo's head against the back wall, their bodies sandwiched and reflecting in the interior mirror. "Is that what you think? That my feelings for you aren't real enough to want a future with you no matter where time sends me?"

Boo's chest rose and fell rapidly as her breaths quickened. "Where time sends *us*. We may never cross paths after this assignment. We're pretending to be FUC agents as much as we're pretending we're engaged."

Willy didn't expect *her* to pull him closer, rise on her tiptoes, or place her mouth over his.

The two transcended time, and the dressing booth disappeared in Willy's peripheral vision.

He lowered his hands and cupped her face, deepening their kiss, tasting strawberries, a sweet, sweet delicacy that only heightened his attraction to Boo. "Delicious."

"I missed this," Boo said against his lips.

A physical connection had never been an issue. But could Willy fuse with Boo mentally? Could they take their relationship to the next level?

Willy forced himself to slow down their passion, but when he pulled away, he lost his footing and reeled backward, tugging Boo with him. Their bodies got caught up in the curtain, and the duo fell to the carpeted floor, literally wrapped up in their embrace.

Boo's giggles healed Willy somehow as she hugged him closer and kissed him again, whispering, "Best fake date ever."

Willy searched Boo's eyes, seeing for the first time a lightness and playfulness dancing in her irises. His belly stirred with that same feeling he'd had in high school. Love and hope.

He laughed until Fanny pulled the curtain off them.

"I am so sorry this curtain tripped you up." The freckle-faced clerk's concerned expression relaxed when she saw they were unharmed. "Allow me to offer a ten percent discount."

Willy stood and helped Boo to her feet.

She ran a hand down the seams and hem, verifying no damage existed on the gown. "The dress is unharmed, thank goodness."

Willy lifted the curtain rod, screwing the extension bar to fit the space. "I'm ready for a fitting when you are, and she'll take the dress."

Willy posed for measurements, a suit fitting him to his surprise, while Boo changed and found shoes. The seamstress adjusted Boo's slit and straps.

"The suit's a perfect fit." Boo rejoined him, a silly grin adorning her face and accentuating her dimpled cheeks as she handed the dress to the salesclerk. "We could spice up this date with a bet to see who solves the case first."

Just like Boo, always playful and competitive, which was A-okay with Willy.

"What's the wager?" he asked.

"How about your van?"

Buzz, buzz, buzz.

Willy broke away first, his cell phone alerting him to an incoming call and distracting him from the bet. For now. He answered, "Alyce."

"Is Boo with you, Willy?" Papers rustled through the receiver.

"Yes, Boo's here," he said.

"She needs to hear this, so put me on speaker," Alyce said.

Willy wasn't keen on broadcasting their conversation

so anyone near could hear. Still, he trusted Alyce to speak in code. He lowered the volume and tilted the phone, placing it at ear level. "Go ahead."

"I received the toxicology report from our victim, verifying my suspicions that a plant-based substance poisoned Zeb."

Boo turned her face toward the receiver. "Plant-based? Tell me, was it Valerian root?"

"How did you guess?" Alyce asked.

"The specific plant has sedative properties." Boo took her package from the salesclerk.

"And more," Alyce continued. "It induces a potent, hypnotic sleep. Valerian plants are so hypnotic that cats are as attracted to them as catnip!"

When Boo's warm complexion turned ashen, he disabled the speaker and lifted the cell to his ear with one hand while lowering Boo to the seat beside the register counter. Something had tripped her up regarding this news. He'd ask her as soon as they had a private moment.

"Alyce, this all makes sense as to why the artifact is so enticing. All we need is access to the event. Once inside, I'll know if the object is there."

"I'm sending a courier with your tickets and other necessities. I have your location in Willow Wisp," Alyce verified.

"That's right. We'll be here for another…" Willy lifted Boo's chin. Her color was still off. He needed to get protein into her before she fainted. "Another few minutes."

"I have your GPS location." Alyce disconnected the call.

Willy tucked that fear into his pocket along with his phone. He took the offered suit bag, thanking the clerk, and then held out a hand to Boo, who securely slid her hand into his as they exited the store. "Next stop is Wispy's."

"Not so fast." Boo motioned to a man flanking Willy's van, his knee bent so his foot rested on the running board.

Willy glanced at Boo, who shook her head. Neither of them recognized the man.

Willy whispered, "Alyce's delivery?"

"I suspect," Boo whispered back.

The duo approached, and Willy examined the stranger, attempting to sniff out what type of shifter he was. Maybe a tricky fox shifter?

The man wore thick-rimmed glasses, and dark lenses blocked his eyes. He worried his tongue over a crack in his lower lip.

"Alyce sent you?" Willy asked.

"Change of plans." The man handed Willy a swollen envelope. "The auction begins in an hour."

CHAPTER
SIX

Don't let 'em see you squirm. Boo checked the tickets inside the envelope for the umpteenth time as she and Willy hurried to the event entrance. She should have been pleased everything was in order as she fanned through the documents, but her quest to locate the Bastet statue hovered in a state of limbo.

Entering the dark web of the auction world, a place she'd sworn off the day she'd found herself behind steel bars, was looking danger in the face.

Would she be recognized?

Would she find the toxin-lathed artifact before someone else fell sick?

If something went wrong, would Alyce know where to find them since they'd ditched their cell phones in the van parked blocks from the alleyway entrance?

"You dressed quickly." Willy adjusted his tie. "We were both lucky the tailor was on site for minor alterations."

"Luck has nothing to do with it." Boo righted her shoulder strap and glanced at her finger to make sure the ring was in place, as it was a size too big.

"A little," Willy rebutted.

Hiss. "If this bank routing number doesn't work when the item comes up for auction, we're screwed."

She needed to return the borrowed jewelry to Alyce as soon as possible, which bothered her less than Alyce's ticket delivery speed, a detail she shoved to the back of her mind. They had the tickets, and she was closer to achieving her goal.

She could taste success. At least she was trying to convince her nerves of that.

"Have faith." Willy rapped his knuckles on the metal door in the dark alley and adjusted his bowtie. "We look amazing and couldn't be more in love."

The arm he yoked her bare shoulders with pressed down on her even though she automatically leaned into him.

She hadn't fully forgiven Willy or herself yet, even though she was moving forward. They'd both wronged the other. She needed more to heal than a conversation, a few moments of laughter, and a risky charade.

A hand-sized window opened. "Password."

Password? Boo looked inside the envelope and strummed through the papers containing the bank information and the map of the auction's entrance.

She tried to moisten her lips and failed. Her tongue felt like desert sand. Her nerves were already frayed, and her past was crowding in, telling her she was on a treacherous path.

"Time's up." The tiny window slid—

Boo poked her finger into the space, her nail stopping the movement. It was now or never if she wanted to complete the mission. "Wait. I have it."

"Keypad is on your right." The window snapped shut.

Sure enough, a keypad hung on the side of the door under a discreet metal cover. Boo lifted the lid, and a neon-lit number pad illuminated the keys.

She hovered her shaking hand over the numbers. Once she was inside, there was no turning back. Had she come this far for confidence to escape her?

"Do you need me to do it?" Willy's shadow rolled over her.

Did she?

No. She wouldn't let fear control her. She forced herself to enter the code: R@v3nsG8

The door clicked and sprang open.

Willy took hold of the handle and opened the door, finding the space inside unguarded. "Mysterious."

"At least we're in," she said with a tremor in her voice.

Willy checked behind them, making sure they were still alone before entering. "Let me go first."

Boo quelled her urge to protest. Willy was a powerful shifter, and brute strength wasn't on her side. She had to work *with* and not against him if they were to pull off team-work, even if she was tuned to working alone.

"Lead the way." She motioned.

A dark hallway led down a flight of stairs, a single bulb hanging above and elongating their shadows.

Willy glanced over his shoulder. "Are you sure this is the place? It doesn't look formal at all."

"Keep going." She brushed a stray curl that had escaped her hastily swept updo.

Her faux confidence was a ploy to convince herself to put one foot in front of the other. FUC agents didn't show fear. Zeb had boldly entered the classroom in search of the thief.

And nearly died.

Keep it together, Boo.

They moved quickly, passing beneath numerous city blocks to the auction house's underground network of hidden rooms.

The city may have been unfamiliar, but the setup was similar. Enter through the industrial part of town and follow the prohibition-era underground network to the ritzy side.

Willy reached behind him, taking up Boo's hand.

She squeezed, appreciating his touch. Willy provided the comfort she'd lacked on her previous private missions. This partnership wasn't so fake after all.

But would they succeed in their mission?

They came upon a line of ten bidders, and the doorman verified the documents before allowing each person to enter.

Boo recognized faces, which sent a chill through her body. Would they remember her? "I can't do this."

Willy put his mouth to her ear. "You know these people."

It wasn't a question. "The woman in the red dress is Ursula Quessin. Ursula is the curator of the Shrines Museum in New York. The gentleman behind her, Mr. Owen Coldspell, is here with his husband, Theodore, owner of Coldspell Museum and an archaeologist. We'll need to keep our eyes on them."

The three were obvious curators of ancient artifacts, but who were the new players who created the glowing lineup? Their presence didn't make entering less risky.

In fact, Boo felt a hiss gather in the back of her throat. Did she smell canine?

A woman cloaked in fur stopped before Ursula, the two ladies acknowledging each other. Ursula handed the other woman a receipt-sized paper, which she pushed into her pocket.

How many backdoor deals would happen tonight? What was on the paper that had the fur-clad woman dashing past Boo to stand behind her in line?

Was she reading the note out loud?

Boo cocked her head. If only she could shift and use her cat ears to home in on the murmured words.

Cemetery.

Plot.

Dig.

The words had once filled Boo's mind when she'd dug up graves to reunite antiques to their rightful families, most belonging to her own. But which cemetery and plot?

A tap on the shoulder spun Boo around.

"Boo Bombay? Is that you?" The woman adjusted her framed glasses, rounded green eyes staring back at Boo and a pinkness riding her ebony cheeks under the floor-length, hooded fur coat.

Boo attempted to mask her shock, but her doe-eyes must have given her away because Ginnie Springston stepped into her personal space.

The woman lived in Willow Wisp. Not only did the woman recognize Boo but she had practically raised Boo as her mother's best friend and neighbor.

Hot paws on a tin roof.

Coming here was a mistake.

Boo would never earn her mother's approval if her mother learned from Ginnie that Boo was involved in illegal dealings. Again.

"I'm sorry," Boo said. "You must have me confused—"

"I don't think so. Boo, you're the spitting image of Cecil-ia," the woman said, whipping her furred hood backward to expose fine lines skirting her eyes and the corners of her ruby lips.

The insistence that Boo resembled her mother sent a quiver down Boo's spine, and a hiss perched on her tongue like a dreaded fart in a packed elevator.

Keep it together!

Boo knew it was a possibility that she'd be recognized, but she didn't expect Ginnie to show up at the black-market event. "I'm sorry, like I said—"

Ginnie touched Boo's hand. "Boo, Boo, it's me, Ginnie. I won't tell your mother you're still gathering family arti-facts. You can trust me to keep this meeting between us."

Boo pulled her hand away, and not because Ginnie noticed the one-carat ring riding Boo's finger. There was no escaping her past, but she tried. "I'm not Boo. I'm, I'm—"

"Miss Emma Greenswald, my fiancée." Willy gathered Boo to his side and wrapped a protective arm around her waist. "Soon to be Mrs. William Tagger, my wife."

The woman squared her shoulders and split her gaze between the two of them as if trying to assign Boo the new name as well as her future married title.

Was Willy crazy? Couldn't he have given an alias? Boo wasn't as lucky as Will to have matured in a doctored way that concealed his identity from townsfolk.

"That's right. William and I are to be married."

Ginnie extended her and then lowered it. "You can't lie to me, Boo. I know you, and I knew the Taggers before they passed."

Boo spun around, turning her back on Ginnie, guessing neither of them were fooling Ginnie.

Rats!

Boo mouthed to Willy, "Emma *Greenswald?* Mrs. Tagger?"

"Later," Willy mouthed, his face as red as a boiled beat.

Would they get in the door before disaster struck?

Ginnie hadn't bought the lie. If she didn't accept Boo's pseudonym, would others when it came time to purchase the Bastet artifact with the fictitious company they represented? Would Boo set herself up to become a target?

Boo and Willy shuffled forward until they reached the doorman.

"Papers?" The doorman scrutinized their IDs. He handed them a numbered bidding stick and opened the door, allowing them access to the event.

The basement was as grand as any five-star hotel banquet hall, with twenty-foot-tall marble pillars, mosaic flooring, and multifaceted crystal chandeliers. Boo lost count of the number of bidders and support staff, who guarded the cloaked items on the stage.

Boo let out a breath. They were in. She didn't know anything about faith, but she remembered a time when she trusted in herself.

Willy placed his hand on Boo's back.

Could he feel the reluctance in her sluggish pace as he guided her toward their seats, which they took in the back row so that they could note the attendants?

Their efforts to appear as a fresh couple in the underground smuggling ring had already failed and they'd barely sat.

"You did well back there." Willy tossed his head toward Ginnie. "Who is she?"

"Someone from my past, Ginnie Springston." She twisted the bidding stick round and round, her confidence in purchasing the statue threatened. "Thank you for the save, even if it made me uncomfortable and didn't change Ginnie's mind."

"That's what partners do for each other." He winked. "I have your back."

No one had ever had Boo's back. She spent a moment inspecting the number on her bidding stick: eight. It was an alarming number. In some cultures, it represented terrible luck.

Death.

She sighed heavily.

"Have faith," Willy reminded her.

Faith was an illusion, one Boo hadn't befriended. Could she trust Willy?

Ginnie came into view, her hand shoved into her coat pocket as she made her way to her seat.

The microphone sent a shrill whine into the crowd. "Testing, testing."

Boo's chest tightened as the auctioneer introduced the first piece, a Ming Dynasty painting, which sold for five hundred thousand dollars.

The buyer didn't cringe at the price.

Willy leaned over, whispering, "I trust Alyce provided an ample budget."

Boo twisted her bidding number. If she were outbid, she would scope out the buyer and create a plan to steal back the piece. It was the only way to ensure no one else got injured.

Instead, she explained, "Egyptian Bastet artifacts aren't as pricey as that painting. Unless someone knows of the statue we're looking for and believes the myth of its time-bending properties."

"Up next is an artifact from Egypt." The auctioneer motioned to the newly uncloaked statue that appeared on a pedestal, centerstage.

The woman in the red dress, Sophia, raised her number.

It was a feline artifact, but not the one Boo came for.

She glanced at Willy. "Are your shifter forms picking up anything?"

Willy sat taller and twitched his nose. "This basement is no more than fifty degrees, so I'm not trusting my goosebumps."

Boo trusted Willy to be truthful about sensing the statue. She no more felt the object than he did. Had the low temperature been set on purpose?

She hugged her bare arms, wishing she could spring fur.

Three more statues originated from Egypt. Ten others were feline-based from various continents. Boo thought the auction would never end as she waited for the Bastet statue to be unveiled.

Over the time it took to present and sell each item, Boo noted Sophia held a particular interest in feline artifacts.

"Sold to number nine," the auctioneer had repeatedly announced. "This concludes the event."

Boo's anticipation withered, and a knot gathered in her tummy. Where was the Bastet artifact? Had bidder nine hoped to find it there tonight as much as Boo and Willy had?

Willy gaped at Boo, both of them disappointed, obviously.

"Well, shit. Now what?" Willy murmured.

"We attend another event until we locate the statue. It's bound to show up." Boo scouted the crowd.

Sophia found Ginnie, who'd shed her coat and motioned toward the back of the room and the cocktail bar.

Boo's curiosity shot through her. She was taking a risk, but that was what FUC agents did, right? "I need to use the restroom. Do you mind waiting here?"

Boo stood from her seat before Willy answered, her

heels rapping against the tiled flooring as she targeted Sophia.

The woman trailed through the dispersing crowd, her cape resembling Red Riding Hood's.

Boo knew the truth. The woman was a wolf shifter whose dress couldn't cover the mutt's stench. No wonder Boo had the urge to hiss when she had made eye contact.

Sophia paused near a marble column, tucking herself behind it but not enough to conceal herself or Ginnie.

Boo stood out like the sun. Why hadn't she worn black like she used to?

Was Willy setting her up to fail like her mother had?

There was no time to debate. Alyce required evidence to solve the case.

She crept closer and placed her back against the opposite side of the column, gluing to the shadows to eavesdrop on the conversation as the crowd grew thin.

"Boo Bombay is here," Ginnie said.

Ginnie hadn't bought Boo's alias. *Yowl!*

"If she's here, where is her mother?" Sophia asked. "Are they working together?"

Working together?

Boo's mother was a righteous saint, critical at best, a Willow Wisp councilwoman, who'd disowned Boo for meddling in stolen artifacts.

"Could be Cecilia nabbed the artifact backstage," Ginnie said. "She's a smart cookie."

"I wouldn't put it past her," Sophia added. "Cecilia comes off as right-hand do-gooder to the mayor of Willow Wisp, but she's been thieving for decades. You need to check the plot and make sure it hasn't been disturbed."

Questions batted Boo's mind, and she twisted her pendant, running her fingers over the smooth stone. Why would her mother disown her when her mom's closest friend was involved in the black market? How closely was Ginnie working with Sophia?

But more importantly, where was Ginnie's fur coat and this plot she mentioned?

Had the thief hidden the Bastet statue with plans to sell the item?

Boo backtracked to the entry doorman. "Excuse me, I'm twisted around. Where's the coat room?"

The bespectacled man shook his head. "Down the hall, take a left."

Boo hurried in the direction of the room, pausing when she spotted Willy scoping out the crowd. He was no longer seated, which meant he'd come looking for her shortly if she didn't return soon, but for now, he was talking with the Coldspells.

Boo teetered, part of her wanting to drag him into her plans. But she resisted. She wouldn't put him in unnecessary danger.

She picked up her pace, checking behind her. No one followed.

She came upon another line, this one to the make-shift coatroom—a skeletal cube with canvas walls.

"Explain to me what the jacket looks like." The clerk held pen to paper.

"It's a coral and green plaid jacket with eagle-feathered embossed gold buttons..."

Boo thought quickly. Ginnie would retrieve her coat soon.

When the attendant leaned forward and wrote the description, Boo entered the glorified closet from the rear.

She expected to find numbered velvet hangers and

neatly hung jackets, but she discovered a nest of wool and fur, each coat piled on top of the others.

Shameful. Boo shook her head. Where to begin?

She pulled one item at a time from the pile, finding the plaid jacket, which stood out like a unicorn among burros. She swooped up the piece, set it closest to the ringed curtain door, and returned to examine the pile.

Boo tapped her cheek. Ginnie's coat was more red fox than gray, right? But among the dozens of participants, Boo had been hyper-focused on the prize when she should have noted details, like the unique making of the coat.

The more layers she uncovered, the more confused she grew.

Double rats!

Boo had faced Ginnie directly. How could Boo become a FUC agent if she couldn't recall the color of a key suspect's fur?

She thrust her hand into one jacket pocket and then the other. Nothing there. She tossed the coat toward the room's opening, creating a second pile as she searched more pockets.

"I'm here for my fur coat," Ginnie said. "It's a Russian sable."

A what? Boo added another thing to learn on her list of things to learn.

"I'll be with you in a minute," the clerk answered, a tinge of irritation in his voice.

Heart jumping, Boo did the only thing she could do to save herself from being caught. She sprouted furred ears and pushed out her tail. A second later, she fell onto her kitty paws, her black fur blending into the pile as she freed herself of her blinding yellow dress.

She searched every pocket, poking her face into the

furry pile, hunting for Ginnie's feline scent among the humans, a benefit of her heightened feline attributes.

Bingo!

She touched the paper with her nose and pulled it out with her teeth. Her eyes blurred as she read the handwritten, coded words.

Triple rats!

"Boo?"

Willy?

She popped her head out of the pile and retook her human form, as naked as a Library Gentlemen's Club stripper in Vegas, or in her case, a feline shifter and Willy's ex-girlfriend.

"You're naked as a jaybird." Willy gawked before wrapping her in a coat.

"What?" she said, nonchalantly. "It's not like this is your first time seeing me without clothes."

Willy brandished a grin. "You're killing me, Boo. You're also not alone in this venture, so what are you doing pillaging the coats?"

"I could ask the same thing." The clerk stood behind Willy, who faced Boo.

Willy stiffened, his face reddening before he yanked Boo close, kissing her passionately. He paused to say, "It's cliche, but it was on my bride's bucket list."

"Well, get a hotel. The coat closet isn't a fuck shack." The clerk snapped the curtain closed upon exiting, swearing under his breath about missing the good old days.

Boo couldn't disregard Willy's disappointment in her or the fact that disappointing him bothered her. He'd asked her to trust him, and she'd let him down. She'd let herself down. "I'm sorry."

"I know you had your reasons. I trust you. Can you trust me from here on out?" He cocked a brow.

His adorable look warmed her shame-filled heart. Faith *was* about trusting her partner, the man she once loved, even if she was relearning how to lean on Willy. "I'll try to do better."

"That's all I'm asking." Willy held Boo's dress, allowing her to step inside.

Once dressed, Boo stood on tiptoes and kissed him, lingering for a moment too long before pulling away. "This is me trusting you."

"With a make-out session? I like it." Willy purred.

She opened her hand. "Tell me you excel in decoding so we can figure out our next clue."

CHAPTER

SEVEN

Willy hustled Boo out of the auction and didn't break until they reached the van and were locked inside. He recognized the coded note, not to the point that he could solve it without help, but he had access to programs as well as the internet through his cell phone.

"You're scaring me," Boo said. "Is the message threatening?"

"I don't think so, but look here." Willy turned his cell phone toward Boo to show her the decoding program he'd mastered at the Academy.

"What am I seeing?" Boo sat forward in her bucket seat. The van was parked in a dark alley, causing her to squint at the screen. "It all looks like gibberish."

To anyone else, the FHPHWHAC wouldn't read CEME-TERY. But to Willy, decoding—the ability to decipher code —was the one thing he'd picked up easily. His mind worked magically, revealing the type of cipher as instantly as any computer program.

Still, he wanted to show Boo how to find online applications if she needed them in the future.

"Encoding—writing code—takes several forms," Willy said. "Substitution ciphers replace letters with other letters or symbols while keeping the order the same. Transposition ciphers keep the original letters but change their order."

"Which means?" Boo tipped the phone to get a better read on the letters.

Willy jabbed a finger at the receipt stub Boo had pilfered from Ginnie's coat, pleased Boo had the foresight to go after a clue, even though she'd done so on her own.

Boo had taught him more about gathering evidence and how to become an investigator— whether she knew it or not—than he'd learned from his Academy professors, who only presented fictional scenarios.

He continued, "An Atbash cipher replaces each letter with its corresponding letter in reverse order so that PLOT would become TOLP. A Pigpen cipher uses symbols made from spatial constructs to represent letters. The Freemasons in the eighteenth century used this type."

"Is that what we have?" Boo looked closer. "It's hard to make out the wonky handwriting."

Luckily, the note was legible. "Coding specifics is one of the optional courses you can take at the Academy."

Boo sighed and smoothed her gown where wrinkles had gathered in her lap. "Perhaps something to look into in the future, but for now, Alyce will want answers. Can you do this or not?"

He should have been offended that Boo challenged him, but this coding business was important to solving their case, and time-crunch or not, he wanted to include his partner. "Boo, I'm giving you a crash course."

She sighed again and placed her hand on his knee. "Go on."

At least she was trying to understand his reasoning.

"Just three more. A Playfair cipher uses an encryption technique. Keywords or phrases are substituted by pairs of letters that are arranged in a box. By shifting the lettered pairs, it spells out a code."

"That type seems as impossible to decipher as the Pigpen type. We could be guessing all night." Boo crossed her legs and folded her arms. "Please tell me this isn't what we have."

"No. Luckily." Willy breathed a sigh of relief. "Nor do we have a Scytale cipher. Otherwise, we'd be staring at a long Roman scroll."

"Then what do we have?" Boo scooted closer, handing him his cell.

Willy leaned into her, sharing the screen. She trusted him with her body. Could she trust his expertise to lead them to the mystery behind the cemetery plot?

"We have a Caesar cipher," he explained. "This type dates back to one hundred BC, and the encoder replaces letters with new letters."

"And the note tells us to order a pepperoni pizza and BYOB?"

Willy smiled, gazing deeply into Boo's pretty eyes. Time stilled as she stared back at him. They connected deeper than at a partner level, even though she was struggling and he was on edge.

Would she take off on her own once he detailed the location written on the note?

"It's not food we'll dig up." He strapped his seatbelt on and started the engine. "Trust me?"

"I do." She fastened her seatbelt.

Willy nibbled on his lip. The last thing he wanted was to spook her. A haunted cemetery was for campfire story-telling. However, the location meant stirring up Boo's past.

"The note provides the plot number at the Willow Wisp Cemetery."

"Wait. What?" Boo twisted in her seat. "I heard Ginnie mention a plot, but I had no idea she was hunting buried artifacts in our town. I thought she meant an ancient gravesite on a continent far from here."

Willy hadn't known Boo was a grave robber until the *Willow Wisp Observer* published her arrest. "I never asked about your incarceration because it wasn't my place, and I was dealing with my own shit at the time."

"You mean understanding chimerism." She placed her hand on his, squeezing.

Horns, fangs, and a smooth fur coat, which replaced his wiry gorilla-shifter hair, and more. "Yeah. But I admit I was curious. Why dig up founding townspeople? Why not leave them to rest?"

Boo dropped her hand and stared out the window, watching the trees race past as Willy sped toward the cemetery.

The mention of graves had hit a nerve with Boo, and he hoped she'd share her reasoning, but she remained silent.

Willy parked and unloaded the shovel and rope from the back of the van.

Boo whistled. "You came prepared?"

They were the first words she'd spoken since his prying question. "Of course. I'm on a mission, same as you are."

He tossed her scrubs and a shirt, a few clothing staples he'd managed to grab back at the Academy. He set the size seven rubber boots on the ground. "These should fit."

She took the outfit, pausing to watch him as he hung up his tux and began to dress.

He pulled button-fly jeans over his hips, a line of belly hair curling over the band, but she'd paused dressing herself. "I had to grab scrubs for you because the commissary doesn't have jeans."

Noticing she was staring as he pulled on his shirt, he said, "What?"

"Nothing. You've matured... nicely."

He gazed over her curvy figure, pausing at her very kissable lips as well as other places he'd never forgotten. "You're still as beautiful as I remember. Now dress so we can solve this case."

The shirt she pulled over her head covered her smile. "Well, I don't think you know the dangers of digging. It's not only cave-ins. The inside of a jail cell, stewing over being charged for your attempt to right wrongs, is the pits."

"I'm trying to understand." After FUC agents rescued Willy from DIC, Willy locked himself in a prison of his mind for a while.

Boo continued, "I'm the good guy. I still believe this even after the courts locked me up for eight long months. Mission or not, I'm not digging up another corpse. I learned my lesson."

Willy hitched the shovel over his shoulder and handed Boo a rope. "Fine. I'll dig. But here's the thing. Maybe the lesson isn't what you learned—to leave the truth buried. It's to learn from your mistakes, to believe in yourself even when it seems impossible."

Boo studied him for a minute, and he gave her that time as they entered the cemetery.

"Willy, you really believe that, don't you?"

He did. "I wouldn't be here if light hadn't shown through my darkest days and led me back to you."

Boo threw her arms around his neck and pressed her lips against his, showing him the wall she'd built around her heart had fallen away. At least that was how he read her affection.

Mist floated about their ankles as if they were standing on a cloud, and the midnight air whipped around their bodies as he welcomed her passion.

She broke away.

He reeled her back. "I want to understand you better. Why dig here all those years ago? What were you trying to prove?"

Boo exhaled. "I don't want to talk about it..."

Only, she did.

And once she started spilling how driven she'd become to learn family's secrets, she kept talking.

"The founding fathers buried their dead *over* my ancestors. Over my heritage. I was looking for proof that our founding fathers claimed our lands and buried their dead on top of my ancestral gravesites. By proof, I mean artifacts."

Willy's body warmed if that was possible. Boo's admissions gave him hope that she'd continue to open up and trust him. "It means a lot to me that you're trusting me with this."

Boo tucked a fallen spiral curl behind her ear. "I found many small items, but nothing absolutely concrete."

Willy clucked. He understood Boo's passion, but her reasoning and her path had holes. "Okay. Let's say you discover the proof. Then what?"

"To be determined." Boo shrugged. "I've found a few artifacts, a knife, which I keep with me always, and jewelry that once belonged to my family, worn by the 1823 founders."

"There could be a logical reason they were buried with

treasures." Willy thought back to his history classes. "Indigenous people often traded with newcomers."

"I know." Boo twirled the end of the rope she carried. "But imagine if you dreamed of joining your people in death and being buried on a grassy knoll overlooking the river and town, only to learn others had claimed the land, erasing the thousands laid to rest generations prior."

Willy took a moment, empathy causing his blood to boil as he dodged headstones with names he recognized as the founding families.

Hell, his parents and grandparents were buried there. "I'd want to return the land to its rightful people, which would be a hard battle to win, but I applaud you for trying."

"It was a mistake." Boo marched off, taking the rope with her and stomping a trail into the darkness before circling back.

Willy attempted to understand her anger, which muddled his actions. He glanced around the grounds. The mist had swallowed up the hillside. From where he stood over the gravesite, Boo was close and safe.

Guess he was digging a hole, and the symbolism wasn't lost on him. He sank his shovel into the soil, peeking at Boo now and then to make sure she hadn't ditched him.

Boo's murmurs reached his ears.

Was she praying, chanting words of respect, singing a folksong, or talking to the dead?

Willy shoveled one scoop after the other. Another shovelful followed the last. Time ticked by, and the moon slid toward the next day, its glow through the mist illuminating the dig site.

He thought about asking for help but resisted.

Boo and Willy had forged a partnership, and sometimes, one partner had to carry the load when the other tired.

Her shadow crawled over him, and he paused, his muscles straining from digging for what seemed like hours even though he was a powerful chimera. He wasn't pissed, but he snapped, "What?"

She held up her cell phone. "Alyce sent a text. Zeb is conscious. She wants to see us at ten in the morning."

Willy breathed relief. Even though they'd yet to secure the statue, that was the best news he'd heard all day. "That's great news. So, you are helping me look for the reason we're here?"

Boo jumped into the hole and reached for the shovel. "I'm ready."

"Without securing a rope?" he barked. "Now that you're down here, how are we getting out of this hole without the tethered rope?"

As if he were a magical beast after creating a four-by-six-by-six hole in the ground, she asked, "Can't you sprout wings and fly us out of here?"

"While I do have wings, yes, they're... well, let's just say that if some men make up for a lack in size by driving large vehicles, then I should own a monster truck of epic proportions."

"Inadequacy and overcompensation. Two of my best friends." She laughed.

The sound gave him butterflies in the pit of his belly, even if the topic was uncomfortable. His chimerism was evolving as much as his new feelings for Boo.

Were they out of the woods in their budding romance? Not a chance.

Could they get caught by a night watchman? Absolutely.

"I'm sorry for snapping," Willy admitted. "I'm six feet under, and the view leaves me vulnerable. Plus, I haven't hit a casket, spotted bones, or anything that leads me to understand the reasoning for coming here other than the name and date of death on the headstone: Tal Basta June twenty-second, 1823."

"June twenty-second, 1823... That's the day Zeb mentioned." Boo gripped Willy's arms. "And I just remembered what it means! That's the year the town was officially founded on the summer solstice."

"Okay..." Willy was having trouble following her logic. "But why is the grave empty?"

"I don't know." She began pacing in the small rectangular space. "It makes no sense that his body is missing. Where else would his family bury him? If he was moved, why leave the headstone here?"

"I agree." Willy tried to make sense of his findings.

"I've found most bodies around the four-to-six-feet range," Boo explained. "But the thing is, this isn't the first empty grave I've found. On some, I've dug up to eight feet into the ground and found nothing, which surprises me every time."

Willy punched his shovel another foot, pulling up only dirt. "What are you thinking that means?"

"I believe the founding fathers crafted fictitious persons to own the plots. Why? I have no idea." She shrugged then shook her head. "Whatever the reason, the real question is this, *why* are we here tonight? Why did Sophia send Ginnie here?"

A swish of material at ground level above them preceded a shadow appearing over them.

Static danced across Willy's skin.

The whites of Boo's eyes flashed as she scuttled into the darkest corner.

Ginnie?

The woman held a rope in her hand. "If one of you climbs out, I can show you exactly why I sent you here before you're both arrested or disappear forever."

Was that a threat?

Willy's scalp itched as his scimitar oryx DNA caused him to sprout three-foot-long horns. Something was up with Ginnie. Why was his skin prickling as if dancing with ants?

"Whoa, whoa! Put away your prongs, sir. I'm here to help Boo," Ginnie said, and one end of the rope rolled down the slope.

"So you say." Willy gripped his shovel and put Boo behind him, protecting her. "How do I know you haven't called the police? Someone ratted out Boo the last time she was here."

"It wasn't me." Ginnie held up her free hand. "It was Cecilia."

Boo gasped and darted around him, showing herself. "My mother?"

"Yes. Cecilia didn't want you to learn the truth about our ancestral land on this hill. See, the dead and fictitious aren't covering a shifter burial site."

"But I've found feline artifacts here." Boo lifted her hand, brandishing her knife etched with feline hiero-glyphics.

"That may be true," Ginnie said. "Our ancestors traded with the founding fathers. Together, the dead rest with their precious valuables."

"Then what am I missing?" Boo kicked at the end of the jute rope.

"Have you ever dug below eight feet? Ten?" Ginnie motioned to the shovel.

Boo shook her head, more of her hair falling from her bun. "No. Once I hit bones or eight feet, I stopped."

"Well, if you *had,* you'd have located something more dangerous than any Bastet statue with similar abilities."

"Like what?"

"A portal."

Boo gasped, and she gripped Willy's arm, her claws suddenly appearing and denting Willy's skin.

"A portal?" Willy's horns lengthened to a fine point, and he snorted. "Right."

"Believe what you wish—or don't." Ginnie swept her hood from her face. "But I'm telling you that the founding fathers were said to use the portal for time-traveling, treasure hunting, and for disappearing. That Bastet statue is a harbinger of sorts, leading the chosen one here so we can finally locate the portal. Of course, getting locked up in a museum would have been a sad conclusion for it. Which is why I had to steal it to ensure it didn't go with that agent to Egypt. Pity I had to poison him in my efforts to get away."

"The FUC agent could have died!" Boo unlocked her grip.

Before Willy could stop Boo or come to terms with the fact that Ginnie had been the thief and the one who'd done Zeb harm, Boo shifted into a black cat, her sleek shape clawing out of the confined space with the help of the rope, leaving her clothes puddled on the earthen floor at his feet along with her boots.

Willy retracted his horns and shifted into his preferred bulked-up puma form. Forgoing getting muddier, he used robust pads and sprouted claws to scale the dig, scooping up their clothes before leaving the hole.

Above ground, he spotted Boo wrestling with Ginnie, who had also shifted. The two black cats were locked in a twist of eight legs and two tails. Fur flew as the two shifters bounced about the graveyard, knocking headstones as they ping-ponged around the cemetery.

Roar!

His warning didn't faze the two.

Willy had taken a backseat with Boo these past two days. He was done with letting her lead. Her decisions affected both. He didn't like trumping her, nor did he want her hurt, but he roared again, only louder this time.

The booming catcall didn't slow down the fight.

Fuck'n A. And here Boo had given him a warning about not losing control.

Willy chased after the ladies, who resembled firework flower spinners, their bodies bouncing off the ground a good two feet and splattering the sod with tufts of hair.

When Boo hissed, Ginnie yowled.

Were they cussing, kitty-style?

Before any real damage happened or the cops showed up, Willy pounced on the more diminutive duo, grabbing Boo by the nape and dragging the hissing feline away from her foe.

He retook his human form, trading his teeth for gentle but firm hands. "That turned nasty quickly."

Boo took her human form and lifted her fists, her tumbleweed hair threaded with grass. "You haven't seen anything. I've been lied to by the two people who were supposed to protect and love me."

Ginnie coughed until she spit a golf-ball-sized hairball, and then she took her human form. "You've always been feisty and curious, which we all know gets our kind killed."

"Our kind? I didn't see you jailed. I didn't see you

doing something to better yourself by protecting the furry kind, when, clearly, you've known more than you've let on."

Ginnie objected. "You don't understand. The Bastet artifact being nearby means the portal could be activated, and *that* means that we're potentially facing a big problem in the form of a resulting black hole."

Though Boo alluded to her training at FUCN'A, Willy didn't believe Ginnie had any knowledge of it, or their mission.

The woman's words made no sense to Willy, and they apparently didn't to Boo either, as she balled her fists at her side and screamed her frustration then tore up the lawn as she paced.

"Are you insane?" Boo shouted. "Can I believe anything you say? You were probably lying about my mother being the one to turn the police on me."

"She did it to save you," Ginnie replied. "To keep her from disappearing without a trace and landing who-knows-where." Ginnie looked to Willy as though he might help her.

"Don't look at me." He held up his hands. "I'm just learning about all of this right now, and to be honest, I have to wonder why a mother wouldn't attempt a conversation to halt Boo from digging up the dead before going to such drastic measures."

"You know how impossible it is to get her to listen to you," Ginnie huffed. "She didn't even want to admit she knew me at the auction. That's why I baited her with the note. That paper was nothing more than a parking stub. I falsified the code and fed the information to Boo when I stood behind her in line."

Boo's shoulders deflated.

Trust came hard for Boo, and this new information about her mother would make it even harder.

"She was a kid," Willy defended. "But not so young that you and her mother couldn't have told her the truth about your worry for her."

"She wouldn't have believed us." Ginny shook her head sadly. "That being said, her mother tried. But in the end, Cecilia decided she'd rather have her daughter locked up than lose her to time like Boo's father."

And there it was—another strange mention of time travel. Willy shook his head. It seemed useless to talk to the woman any further. "Come on, Boo, let's get out of here." He tossed her the clothes he'd brought up with him while he dressed in his own.

"You can't leave before you have this," Ginnie offered.

Willy didn't expect Ginnie to produce the wrapped statue. One look at it caused his skin to prickle like it was on fire.

To his surprise, Ginnie handed it over to Boo, who took it gently into her arms and cradled it with a tenderness that brought a tear to his eyes.

"Why are you just handing it over?" Boo asked.

"Because it belongs to you." Ginnie shrugged. "But before you had it, I needed to make sure you heard me, that you understood my warning. Do *not* let it fall into the wrong hands. And more importantly, you should *never* go back to digging in this town."

Ginnie left them standing there as she disappeared into the mist.

"Let's return it to the Academy," Willy suggested, thrilled that they'd succeeded in their mission. He couldn't wait to hand the statue over to Alyce.

Boo glanced up at him. "I have an apartment close by.

We aren't due to meet Alyce until ten, so we could go there and shower."

"Okay. I can drive us there." Willy gathered his shovel and rope, leaving the hole behind, and they walked back to the van.

He considered Boo's mental state. Nothing about obtaining the statue felt climactic. "You okay?"

"Not really." She climbed into the van clutching the artifact. "I have a lot to think about."

"That's understandable." The information Ginnie had given Boo about her mother's role in her arrest had to weigh heavy on her.

They rode in silence all the way to her place, but when he parked, Boo spun in her seat.

She took up his hand. "I don't want to be alone for what remains of the night."

"Neither do I."

He followed her into the apartment and closed the door behind him.

CHAPTER

EIGHT

Inside her Willow Wisp apartment, Boo wrestled with the information she'd gleaned from Ginnie as she looked over the statue.

But she didn't feel like celebrating.

The elation of obtaining the artifact was clouded by the fact that her mother had been the one to betray her years ago.

Not only that, but she had a choice to make. Stick to her original plan of stealing the artifact for herself, to return it to her family, or allow Willy to bring it back to Alyce? He was on a high, excited that he'd accomplished his first mission, proving he was on his way to becoming a FUC agent.

And she didn't want to take that away from him.

She also wasn't sure that she cared about returning the artifact to her family. She'd been so convinced about its rightful home, but now, after what Ginnie had revealed, she wasn't so sure it mattered anymore.

Actually, not much of anything seemed to matter

anymore. Not after she'd learned the reason her mother rejected her: to protect her.

Not that she bought her mother's efforts.

The one-bedroom apartment closed in on her. Trying to ground herself, she glanced down, but her muddy boots clouded her view, the dirt as thick as Cecilia's betrayal.

Boo jostled the artifact, which seemed to sizzle in her hands. It seemed to call to her, and Willy stared, mesmerized.

"This statue is a pain in the ass," she commented, setting it down. "I can't wait to hand it off to Alyce."

"Is there anything I can do for you?" Willy asked, seeming to understand she had a lot on her mind.

"I don't know. I need to shower." She stood in the lighted entryway, the rest of the apartment as dark as a tomb, and her heart, if she was honest.

"I need one, too." Willy removed his boots and set them in the shoe tray adjacent to the front door.

Would he join her in the shower?

Was she ready for that, and possibly more?

He stepped toward her. "Let me help take your mind off of whatever is brewing behind your pretty eyes."

Her mother's betrayal wrapped her like black widow cobwebs and poisoned her. She admitted, "I'm nauseous and numb. I can't get my mother's disloyalty off my mind."

Willy ran his hand down her arm. "I bet I can change that."

There was no tentativeness in his hungry gaze. He'd known Boo long before today, knew her silence was a cry for help. But she cautioned herself. It would be so easy to allow her heart to embrace him again, but that wasn't what this was. Willy had a future, a plan to be a globe-trotting agent. This? Only sex. Nothing more.

She warned, "This doesn't mean we're together, together. You can leave any time."

"Whatever you say, Boo." He picked her up, walked toward the kitchen counter as if she were weightless, and set her on the white granite, removing her boots. He used a kitchen towel to remove the mud crusted to her feet. "I know *exactly* what this is."

Was she that coldhearted?

Or was he using her to meet his own needs?

Did he also crave comfort rather than disappointment?

Did it matter when he'd leave after graduation?

He lifted her shirt and let it fall to the laminate vinyl flooring. Making quick work of her tied waistband, he tugged her pants off and added them to the pile. He licked his lips.

Full, kissable lips. Boo had always loved kissing Willy. The softness the gorilla shifter controlled behind his brute strength never ceased to amaze her. The chimera he'd become was no less spectacular.

She was a refined feline, even in her human form, and Willy's chimera strength could break her into pieces.

She massaged his muscular shoulders, exploring his corded, sinewy physique. "You're magnificent."

He peeled off his shirt and cast off his jeans, revealing dual cocks, which stood erect and ready inside his underwear. "Don't build me up too much. It's been a while."

She didn't expect her already choked-up voice to catch in her throat as she clung to his words. Had she been the last person he'd had sex with since their breakup four years ago?

Would she be his first all over again?

He covered himself with a hand. "I'm different now. I don't know how this is going to work."

She slid off the counter and moved closer, placing her hand over his before dropping to her knees. "I do."

She blamed her heightened desire to please him on the magical statue as she pulled down his tented underwear and took him in her hands. Each member was long, thinner than she remembered, but together more than ample, and the left was slightly shorter than the right.

The spongy tips played along her lips as she teased one and then the other before taking the first into her mouth.

Salty, buttery, the precum at the tip was how she remembered. Willy was her guy, and fate had somehow miraculously brought them together to soothe each other, which was a jump after the trauma they'd both suffered.

She glanced up at him, catching the need flying out of his gaze. She sucked, earning an eye roll from him before he clasped her shoulders and pulled her to stand.

"You'll make me come if you keep that up," he growled.

"Kinda my plan." She winked playfully, a first for her in a long time.

"I thought you'd get grossed out seeing me. Altered."

"You mean double the pleasure?" she teased, and her core quickened.

"I'm not a gum commercial."

He most certainly was not. The turn of events blew her mind, and desire had crept in, slowly at first and then wholly, the pain and web of betrayal unraveling. "No. You're a wow."

"You're pretty wow yourself." He pressed his lips to hers.

She motioned to his cocks as if saying, *mind blown*, and then a tiny voice stole her smile.

He'll leave.

No. Love is forever.

He tugged her forward, a growl percolating in his chest. "Now, let me erase your mind's background noise."

Before she rebutted, he melded his lips against hers. A quick maneuver and her bra released her breasts. Willy slid one strap off her shoulder and then the other, letting the lacy garment fall to their feet. He used his thumbs to shimmy down her panties.

She kicked her thong into the pile and followed his lead, tucking her fingers into his underwear band and using a seesaw motion to guide them to the ground.

When they were both bare, he hoisted her over his shoulder, giving her a pat on the butt that sent tingles scattering across her body, and the sensation had nothing to do with the magic emanating from the statue.

He stalked into the darkness. "Bathroom?"

"Turn here."

He smacked her ass again, earning a pleasure-filled yip from her before he flipped on the lights and set her down in front of the shower.

"Stay put," he ordered, his mouth crooked with a sexy smile.

The water rained from the ceiling showerhead.

Willy tested the temperature. "It's perfect."

So was he. Everything he'd done so far had pulled Boo to the present.

The room steamed.

Or it could have been her view through her misty gaze.

He lifted her again and wrapped her legs around his waist.

The rock-hardness of his penile duplication pressed against her pussy, and she squirmed, trying to align herself.

The cool shower tiles barely quenched the inferno inside her when Willy backed her against the wall.

She wrapped her arms around his neck. "This is nice."

He lifted her by her thighs, teasing her with his cocks by shifting his hips. "I-I don't know how this works."

So, this *was* his first time after undergoing a mutation. Like snakes and lizards, had the mad scientist used squamate DNA when he infected Willy with chimera DNA so he'd become as unique as her?

A twist of Fate.

To quell his trepidation, she promised, "I know exactly how to make you feel like you were born for me."

"Do you now?" he purred.

She lowered her arms, guiding each of his penises to her openings. She'd been born with didelphys, a rare condition of having a double uterus. Though Willy hadn't noticed when they were together before, her vaginal canal actually was split in two by a thin membrane, and Willy had somehow morphed into her perfect sexual partner, having diphallasparatus.

What were the odds?

She didn't want to let him see her tears of joy, but he brushed them away with the sweep of his thumb.

"Are you sure you want me?" he asked.

Consent was never in question. "Yes, but the reason for my tears isn't what you think."

"Tell me," he said.

She held his gaze, forcing strength into her posture and her words. "I let my anger and shame keep me from loving the one person who meant the world to me, the person who's my perfect match. I've wasted so much time, and there's no way to get back what we had or backfill the gap."

Her admission lifted a weight from her shoulders. She didn't know if Willy still pictured a future with her—one filled with traveling and then returning to Willow Wisp when they were finally ready to settle down and start a family.

She didn't pry. She refused to let prior trauma enter her new world.

But she admitted her regret. "Imagine what we could have been."

"I'm holding on to what we *are*. Boo, you didn't lose anything." Willy kissed her. "You didn't lose me. You won't. I'm not going anywhere."

She tightened her legs around his hips and pulled him deeper into her, fusing their union as he filled her up in more ways than sexually. "I love you, Will."

He hadn't told her he loved her back, but she took his eagerness, how he possessed her body, as a sign that, together, they'd fulfill new goals and dreams.

That, together, they'd solve significant problems.

She wasn't sure who started to move first, whether she lifted her body, stroking him with her cores, or if he lifted her with his powerful arms. She clung to him, the burning heat inside her ramping up to something explosive.

"God, you're amazing," she said on a gasp.

The walls of the shower disappeared. Either that or she went blind from the orgasm that rushed forward.

He braced a hand against the wall and kept a steady rhythm. "Come for me, kitten."

Her body seemed to float above their two as if they'd been there before—two souls coming together, repairing old wounds and mending hearts.

She rode the wave of ecstasy he endowed her with, euphoric waves pounding through her, mounting a cosmic tsunami that raced forward toward an apex of need before shattering into a trillion tiny pleasure pulses. "Don't stop."

He met her needs until she fell against him.

Maybe he felt her quivering core or sensed she wasn't ready to unlock herself from around him. He held her, carrying her from the shower to her bedroom, their bodies wet as they fell onto the bed, where he reinserted himself.

"I don't want to stop," he said, a smoldering look in his dark gaze.

"Then don't. I want you, Will. All of you. Even the parts that you don't understand about yourself. I accept you, dicks and all." She raked her nails down his back, not enough to slice but just enough to heighten his enjoyment.

His gaze darkened, he hardened, and the second orgasm they shared quaked her soul.

"Boo!" Willy collapsed on top of her.

His weight grounded her to reality—an uncomplete but healed reality.

There was only one thing left to do.

Yes, Boo was ready to face her past.

Willy lay beside her, drawing lines with his finger down her arm, and catching his breath. "What are you thinking about? I hope it's not running."

"Not a chance. What we just shared was epic." She held his half-lidded gaze. "But I have to deal with my mom's betrayal somehow."

He propped his head on his arm. "What happened between the two of you?"

Boo hadn't forgotten that Willy was dealing with the nightmare DIC put him through during her time in jail.

She explained, "Mom walked away when I got arrested. I don't see why she abandoned me, comparing me to what my father did to her. I don't understand how she made peace with ostracizing me."

"Leaving you homeless." Willy huffed, a snarl curling his upper lip.

Boo suspected he was as irritated by her mother's actions as she was. That and attempting to understand her pain.

Boo asked, "Alyce told you about finding me on the streets?"

"No. Not exactly." His hair fell across one eye when he shook his head. "Alyce would never betray a secret."

Then how had Willy found out? Unless... "You did your own investigation?"

"I would have rescued you myself if Alyce hadn't stepped in. When I saw you, knowing you hated me—"

"I never hated you," she shot back.

It was the truth. She could see that clearly now. She'd been angry at herself for pushing everyone away and blind to those who cared about her.

He cocked his head. "I don't think your pride would have let you accept my help."

Willy was right. She had been angry at the universe. Was her mother as well? Is that why she'd turned her back on Boo?

"So, Alyce showing up and offering me a place at the FUC Academy was your idea." She mimicked him caressing her, touching the muscles that strained his exterior.

"I might have influenced her a bit, yeah. But she still had to vet you and had the last say," he admitted.

Rapture swept Boo up, and she smiled.

Willy had acted selflessly even during his crisis.

She burrowed into his chest, her body still humming from making love. She pictured waking up to him for the rest of her life, and her feelings for him multiplied as the waning moon kissed the sleepy sunrise.

His soft snores wafted around her, and the weight of his body settled against hers.

Boo whispered, "Sweet dreams, my love."

She understood her next move and pictured it as if she were viewing it on IMAX.

No future with Willy existed if she didn't make peace with her mother.

Boo wasn't in an exceptionally forgiving mood. Not yet. But she was ready to face the one person she'd tried to prove herself to all her life.

She had four hours before meeting Alyce at ten.

She'd be back in bed in an hour without Willy missing her. Then they could start their life together.

She understood power. Her mother's phantom presence had orchestrated Boo's whole life. It was time to confront Cecilia and take back control.

Boo slid out from under Willy, dressed, and quietly left the bedroom.

As she headed to the door, the artifact drew her attention.

She wasn't sure why, but she decided to take it with her.

One hour. What could go wrong?

NINE

Boo rapped her knuckles on the front door of her childhood home, certain her mother was home. It was close to seven in the morning, and Mom's sedan was sitting in the driveway. Boo's pulse sounded in her ears, and her mouth dried. She was doing the right thing: preparing a future free of old baggage.

Packed with relevant knowledge of her mother's betrayal, Boo lifted the lion-shaped door knocker, the brass as etched as her mother's surprised expression when she opened the door.

"Mom."

"Boo." Cecilia wedged her body between the door and the door's molding, the hem of her bathrobe fluttering about her mocha calves. Her bonnet crumpled against the doorframe. "What took you so long?"

Years of self-doubt and blame edged the perimeter of Boo's mind, and that was all she allowed. "I'm here now. Someone dear to me convinced me to make peace with you and to put my past behind me."

"It's not that easy." Her mother stepped onto the porch

and closed the door behind her, adding a judgy gaze. "Expecting you and handing out forgiveness after you lived like an alley cat, shaming the entire family, won't be easy."

It was just like Cecilia to sway things to make her look good when she'd been digging up graves along with Ginnie.

Was that how Cecilia gained her executive place on the Willow Wisp governing board?

Boo waved her hand in dismissal. "I don't want forgiveness. I don't even think I need it, considering I was only following in your footsteps."

"Following me? That's absurd." Cecilia narrowed her green eyes and lifted her manicured index finger. "You don't have a clue what I do. I'm not a criminal, a betrayer, and a selfish puss."

A moment passed before Boo answered, "I thought recovering and returning family artifacts to their rightful owners *was* justice."

"Justice, is that what you call it?" Cecilia *pffted*. "Anyway, why are you here? What do you need, money?"

"No." Boo gathered her thoughts as she anxiously twisted the phony engagement ring on her finger. She'd left it in the van before she and Willy had started digging in the cemetery, and she'd put it back on when they'd returned. Of course, her mother made no comment on the fact that her daughter wore an engagement ring.

Whatever.

Shouldn't her mother see her like Willy did? Shouldn't Cecilia see that Boo had changed for the better, regardless of her muddy attire?

Cecilia blew out a breath as if she was tired of Boo already. "My last words to you were to keep out of the cemetery, but no. Not Boo. She didn't listen. She's not listening now. Just like your father."

Boo's belly cramped like a gut punch. This was her mother, sharp-tongued and still angry, just like Boo suspected.

Her mother wasn't outright rejecting Boo, but her disappointment gathered creases on Cecilia's brow.

If Boo allowed herself to crumble, her mother would have an eternal hold on her, something that would ruin Boo's future.

Boo settled for honesty. "We've never seen eye-to-eye."

"Truer words have never been said." Cecilia checked her nails. "What will the neighbors think? I never wanted a criminal to come knocking looking for handouts."

"I'm not a criminal—" Boo paused. She would not explain herself.

Her mother placed the back of her hand on her forehead. "You've taken enough from me already."

Boo took a step back. Her mother would always play the victim. That was a given. "I was never good enough for you. I almost wonder if you enjoyed the fact that I was independent, because it gave you the perfect opportunity to rid yourself of me. Tell me, how much did you enjoy calling the police on your own daughter?"

Her mother's eyes widened, and she righted her bonnet, the same one she'd worn years ago with the little pink mice dancing around the band.

Some things never changed.

But Boo had.

"You know?" Cecilia hissed. "Who told you? Ginnie?"

"Yes." Boo stood taller, not so much in defiance or defense but to show her mother that she was no longer affected by her mother's unhealed trauma. "I met Ginnie tonight in the cemetery, and she filled me in on your little coverup."

"She wouldn't betray me," Cecilia scoffed.

Me. Me. Me.

Boo was tired of arguing, but she should have expected nothing less than an unresolved past.

She should have stayed put, in bed with Willy.

"Tell me this, Mom. How many more secrets are you keeping from me?"

Her mother laughed, her mouth opening wide and flashing teeth and a lopsided uvula. "Why would I tell you? I keep secrets away from vandals and felons."

Was Cecilia charging Boo a criminal?

Okay, the charge was earned.

Boo looked at the withered features her mother displayed. They not only showed in her face but also in her stature and attitude. Boo registered shame in her mother's gaze.

If Boo didn't keep to the right path, she'd end up like Mom.

Boo's cell phone rang.

She pulled the device from her pocket and answered without glancing at the caller ID. "Willy, I can explain—"

"It's Alyce Cooper, and I've moved the meeting to eight a.m. It's urgent, Boo." The phone crackled. "Return to the Academy ASAP."

"I need to pick up Willy."

"Not necessary. He's on his way." Alyce ended the call.

Boo stared at her phone, her heart sinking, knowing that Willy wouldn't be happy, waking up and finding both her and the statue gone.

Boo pocketed the phone. She had no idea what Alyce's urgency was about, but as she left her mom standing on the porch, she felt sorry for her mother and the anger that had aged her.

Her mom called out, "All you've done is run from the truth and cause me grief, just like your father."

The only truth Boo ran from was her mother's continued deception and backstabbing ways. Boo dashed to her car and called Willy on the way, but the call went to voice mail.

She tried again and left a message. "I have the statue. I'll meet you at the Academy. I love you."

She sped forward, praying Willy would understand why she'd left, hoping he would give her time to explain where she'd gone, even if she hadn't made amends with her mother.

But in the back of her mind, all she heard was her mother's voice.

You're the criminal, a betrayer, and a selfish puss.

TEN

"The same shit from Boo!" Willy barked under his breath as he stalked the hall toward Alyce's office. He'd been mumbling how used he felt after waking up alone and discovering the missing statue all the way from Boo's apartment in Willow Wisp to the FUC Academy.

The urgent phone call from Alyce hadn't only jarred him from his post-coital, cloud-nine dreamscape. Boo's absence had ripped his heart from his chest, and that pain hadn't eased by the time he reached Alyce's office without Boo.

He glanced up and down the hallway. Where the hell was that grimalkin? Where was the artifact? Who could he trust? Should he wait for Boo before meeting with Alyce?

Damn it. He clenched his fists.

Even though Boo had given him the slip, he couldn't help but wonder if she was okay, and worry twisted his insides.

Alyce sat at her desk, intermittently snacking on a carrot chip, combing through a stack of filed COC forms that the Conflict Resolution and Situation De-escalation counselors submitted for her review.

It wasn't so long ago that he'd had a complaint filed against him when he was a newbie EJAC—an Experimental Juvenile Active Cadet.

Occasionally, Alyce scrolled her signature on the page.

Impatience drove him to make himself known. "You wanted to see me, Alyce?"

She glanced up, spotting him hovering on the threshold. "Oh, you made good time."

He'd sped like an antelope chased by a cheetah.

His graduation depended on him passing Forensics 101, and he hadn't forgotten he owed Alyce his loyalties for meeting his personal goals.

"Take a seat. This is important." Alyce motioned to one of two chairs facing her desk.

He did as she asked, chastising himself for nearly throwing away those goals for dreaming about staying in Willow Wisp and playing house with Boo.

He'd been stupid. He'd allowed Boo to play him like a monkey in a tree.

"Alyce, did you reach Boo?"

"She's on her way and should arrive shortly." The director pulled an envelope before her.

As if on cue, Boo entered, shooting Willy a soft look as she handed the artifact over to Alyce as well as the ring she'd borrowed.

Willy's heart clenched.

"The statue is dangerous," Boo said. "Make sure anyone who touches it uses lead gloves... or is a feline shifter."

Alyce nodded, sliding the ring onto her finger before donning a thick pair of gloves. She picked up the artifact and walked it over to an office closet, where she placed it in the safe inside. After securing the object, the director retook her seat.

Willy felt no less deceived as Boo sat beside him.

"I understand you two bet on who'd deliver the statue." Alyce split her gaze between the two guilty parties before letting it land on Willy.

Fuck'n A. Had Alyce overheard Boo asking him to wager his van? If so, what else did she know about what had transpired between him and Boo? The mind-blowing sex? Boo telling him she loved him? Him not saying it back? Who was the bigger-looking idiot?

No wonder Boo left their love nest.

"Willy, pay Boo, so we can discuss your failed assignment," Alyce said.

Failed? They'd delivered the statue.

Boo did.

Willy's skin twitched from head to toe. Ginny had handed the artifact to Boo, so technically Boo was the one who'd recovered it.

But the way she'd stolen it out from under him, while he slept, no less, rankled him.

Screw her. Willy wasn't letting Boo off so easily. Boo was in this game for her own reasons, and she'd never be a team player.

He dug his keys out of his pocket, the plastic Academy charm having a torn corner. It seemed appropriate since his heart had ripped.

"We never shook on it, so the wager is moot." Boo waved away the key. "Besides, you're angry, but I can explain."

"Save it." He gave her his profile. She'd played him last night. Betrayed him as much as DIC had manipulated him into the van and then broken his body and spirit.

That shit hurt, and Willy was done. Done, done, even if he also loved her.

He turned the conversation back to Alyce. "So, Director Cooper, what's the emergency?"

"You missed your pickup." Alyce pulled a white letter-sized envelope off her desk and extracted two tickets, the gold embossed lettering reflecting the fluorescent ceiling light. "Now, I'm pleased you managed to obtain the artifact, but as far as conducting yourself like actual agents, you dropped the ball. Agents need to check in with their superiors and advise them of changes, keep them apprised of the mission status, receive approval before going in a different direction."

Alyce accused them of avoiding the delivery of the tickets? No, they'd followed her instructions. *Mostly.*

"Wait a minute." Willy held up his hands as if saying whoa. "We met with the delivery person and attended the auction. That's how we tracked down the stolen statue."

He explained the gist of their sting last night. Alyce didn't need to know everything. Although she most likely already did. Llama shifters were intelligent and observant, attributes Alyce had honed.

"That's not possible. I have the tickets right here." Alyce held them up.

Willy expected Boo to take over the convo, but she sat with her hands folded in her lap.

She was impossible to read.

He crossed his arms and ankles, stewing.

"The last time we talked," Boo said, "you told us you had our GPS, which will confirm—"

"Nothing." Alyce punched into her standing position. She turned her computer monitor their way, presenting a map of town. "This is where you were when we spoke, at the Bluetique. The map details your GPS location for the evening. Notice your location versus the location of the auction I intended you to attend."

"I don't understand," Boo said. "Who handed us the tickets for the auction we *did* attend?"

"You better believe I intend to figure that out," Alyce replied. "In the meantime, the two of you need to take these tickets and attend the event, as originally planned."

"Why attend an event when we have the prize?" Willy asked.

Alyce spun her computer back around. "According to Zeb, when he found the artifact, he determined a stone was missing from the piece. He believes someone local possesses the gem, which legend says would make the statue more powerful."

Boo sank her nails into his leg.

"Ouch." Willy jumped.

"Sorry." Boo removed her hand. "It's just that wasn't expected. So, Zeb thinks that someone from Willow Wisp possesses this stone, but whom? There are over a thousand people living in the cozy town."

"I'm guessing that's correct, which is why I want the two of you to go to a reception at the Willow Wisp Museum. Record the participants. Catalog their jewelry. Look for a heart-shaped gem of unknown color. I assume your feline DNA will pick up any oddities, similar to your innate reaction to the statue."

Willy took the tickets and shoved them into his pocket. The task was impossible.

He and Boo were barely talking. Now, they had to hunt for jewelry-wearing guests—like looking for a bee in a colony of beehives.

He still didn't trust Boo, or her role in this power grab.

Willy huffed. "Listen, Alyce, there's something you need to know."

"Willy, don't," Boo warned.

He'd had it with secrets. Secrets could get people killed.

"When we followed a clue to the Willow Wisp Cemetery, we ran into an old friend of Boo's. She revealed that Boo's mom was the one who turned her in. With that much bad blood between them, maybe it's not so wise for Boo to continue working on this investigation."

There. He'd said what he had to say.

Alyce leaned forward, her elbows on her desk, tightening the distance between them. Her eyes landed on Boo as she asked, "And that's where you were this morning, confronting her?"

"Yes, ma'am," Boo admitted, ducking her head, and her cheeks flushed with color.

Willy felt compassion toward Boo, realizing that the meeting must not have gone well.

"Well, whether or not you continue is up to you. Do you want to be let off the case?"

Boo's head snapped up, her eyes blinking in shock. "You mean, I have a choice?"

"Of course you do. If you feel up to it, then I trust you to be able to focus on finding the stone Zeb is looking for."

"You trust me..." Boo murmured as she stood. "Thank you, Director Cooper. You won't regret this."

"We'll report our findings after the auction Friday night," Willy added, standing alongside Boo.

"Good. Now, if I'm not mistaken, the two of you already used your outfits at the first auction, so you'll need attire to present yourself at the upcoming function. Best you make your way back to the Bluetique." Alyce continued to hum.

Boo followed Willy into the hallway, letting Alyce's office door close behind her.

From Boo's twisted expression, he understood her frustration. Perhaps not as much as his when it came to personal problems, but they were synced about the mission.

"Don't be mad at me." Boo blinked up at him.

It was already Thursday, and the solstice was hours away. How would they pull off such a feat?

"Why shouldn't I be? I specifically asked you yesterday to trust me. To not run off without me again." His hair flopped about his eyes. "What the hell were you thinking leaving this morning without so much as a goodbye or a note?"

"It's not what you think," Boo defended. "I just wanted some closure. I was foolish enough to think maybe I could fix things with my mother. I mean, if I can't trust my own mother, how can I trust you?"

Willy dragged her down the hall away from passersby. "Don't you see how it's the same thing all over again with you running off and doing your own thing?"

"I did it for us." Boo kicked at a seam in the tile. "I mean it's why I thought I was doing it. Turns out, speaking to my mother didn't help one iota."

He lifted her chin. "We're supposed to be partners, Boo. You didn't think leaving would bother me? That I wouldn't think the worst of you or maybe believe that something bad happened to you?"

"Listen…" She pressed her face into his palm. "We need a truce to work together. And I need to accept that I'll never have my mother's forgiveness. She doesn't have that capability."

Trust in faith.

He fucking hated his thoughts.

Things were shaky now. Would there be anything left to hang on to when this was over?

ELEVEN

Willy led Boo to an alcove where they could talk freely. "I take it that whatever happened when you saw your mother is still unfinished between you."

"That's an understatement." Boo rolled her eyes. "I barely got two words in before she blamed me for her miserable life and tarnished reputation. I swear she cares more about her public image than me."

Willy may have felt betrayed by Boo, but she'd allowed herself to be vulnerable with him.

She trusted him now, clutching his hand. Was he just a partner for the time being? Or was he something more?

Blind faith.

"I'll meet you back at the dress shop," he said as they headed toward the parking lot.

Once inside his van, Willy fired up the engine and sped away from the Academy, and Boo remained heavy in his thoughts. He tried to calm his nerves even though his heart was running laps behind his ribcage. It was barely nine in the morning. What could go wrong between the Academy and town?

Flat tire.

Herd of steers.

Grass fire.

All right, all right. He shut down his racing mind.

Perhaps he shouldn't have mused on such a silly question. No sooner did he cross into town than he was greeted by a police siren and flashing lights.

"What the hell?"

He pulled over, and when the officer approached, he only glanced at the license and registration Willy offered.

"Willy Tagger?"

"Yes," Willy replied, knowing he hadn't been speeding. "What is this about, officer?"

The officer took a step backward. "I'm going to ask you to please step out of the vehicle and come with me."

Willy wanted to object, but the officer placed his hand on his weapon, and Willy realized the officer wasn't in any mood for discussion.

"There has to be some kind of mistake," Willy said, stepping out of his vehicle and placing his hands on his head to allow the officer to cuff him.

"If there is, then we'll clear it up at the station."

Willy tossed a look over his shoulder. "Can you at least tell me what this is about?"

"We received a report from Cecilia Bombay that she was robbed this morning."

Willy's mouth dropped open in shock. "And she said *I* did it?"

The officer said, "You and her ex-con daughter, Boo, yes."

With that, the officer was done talking. He guided Willy to the police car and opened the door, pushing Willy's head down as he got in.

The road to town was lined with re-election billboards. Although Willy wasn't a politician, he mulled over ways to win his freedom.

They arrived at the station just as another police cruiser was parking. Willy's heart sank as he saw the officer of that vehicle pull Boo out of the backseat.

"My mother's gone too far this time!" Boo shouted.

Willy's officer helped him out of his car, and Boo caught sight of him. Her mouth dropped open.

Willy assured Boo, "We'll call Alyce and get this handled."

"Shut it," his officer instructed.

The four of them entered the police station. Willy was guided to the right, while a female officer ushered Boo left.

As the distance grew between them, and before Boo disappeared from his view, she called out, "Save yourself, Willy. Don't worry about me."

Only he did.

The holding cell was metal, cold, and hard. A dark stain encrusted the base of the seatless toilet. Willy pressed his face between the bars. He was sure Boo's holding cell was just as awful, and he feared that she'd be taken back to her last stint in the clink.

He had to free Boo. She didn't deserve punishment. "I need to make a call. Hey! It's the law. Let Boo go. She's innocent."

His shouts fell on deaf ears, and he retook his seat on the lumpy bunk, hanging his tired head. Where had he gone wrong?

He should have stayed far away from Boo Bombay.

Impossible. He damn well cared for Boo.

No, he *loved* her.

And loving someone didn't mean giving up on them when things got complicated.

The sun through the high window stretched the shadows of the bars, resembling three headstones.

Headstones.

Tal Basta

June 22, 1823.

The bedspring complained when Willy shifted his weight.

Back at the cemetery, Willy had taken the name on the headstone at face value. But suddenly, he realized Tal Basta wasn't a person's name at all. The ancient city northeast of Cairo in the eastern Nile Delta was noted in his history class.

Tal Basta or Tell Basta, Per-Bastet, meant "The Domain of Bastet," which linked the cemetery headstone to the golden phallus with the cat head currently locked in Alyce's safe.

As a history buff, Willy was sure of that.

Not only that, but Zeb had whispered coordinates to Boo, which Willy needed to verify but he was pretty sure they led to some vital clue within Tal Basta.

Certainly, the graveyard held other clues to help spell out Willy's next move.

Including reaching out to DILDOS, the Detective Inter-webs Looking and Decoding Operating System, a multiple hacking and search function tool developed by fellow Academy members.

Willy glanced at his watch when he spotted the sun slipping toward the evening. Only it wasn't just any date. It was June twentieth, which meant he had forty-eight hours to skate this cell and prove the existence of the portal before the summer solstice struck on June twenty-second.

He lunged to the bars fronting his cell, expecting an impossible escape through an army of officers.

The lone officer had his feet on his desk and a phone pressed to his ear.

The man was preoccupied, which shoved Willy into gear.

"It looks like multiple felonies are in my future," Willy muttered.

Willy inhaled a cleansing breath. He'd mastered transforming into a big cat. He'd always been on the large size, but cats were known for being liquid.

Willy's body shook and his bones shrank as he pictured the perfect feline.

He gritted through the pain of transformation. With that discomfort, he accepted that he'd been changed into a chimera for this purpose, that somehow Fate had intervened, making him the chosen one. At least for now.

He closed his eyes as he fell to all fours. Black fur sprouted, overtaking his skin. His whiskers twitched, and he yowled, catching his sleek form in the steel bars' reflection. He stretched his lanky back and checked over his shoulder, his long, black tail reminding him of Boo's.

Willy wasn't her, of course. But he'd used her Bombay breed's form as a template—a gorgeous feline if he said so himself.

He dragged his clothing to the bed and stuffed it under the mattress, which appeared no less lumpy than it had before. Of course, someone would discover his clothes, shoes, and watch, but he'd be long gone by then.

He squeezed through the bars and sprinted through the building. When an officer opened the door, Willy sprang toward freedom.

Once outside, he took note of his surroundings, spotting bushes that fronted the building. He sprinted toward the women's side of the jail, not more than fifty feet from where he'd been, and made his way around the building to the back where the jail sat behind the offices.

His heart beat a thousand times a minute when he caught Boo's scent.

She was inside, behind the block wall, her tiny jail cell window just a foot below the roof's edge.

Counting the blocks, he measured how to reach her window. If he dangled from the roof line, he could find purchase on the sill.

Luckily, there was a wood fence butting up to one side of the jail. He climbed the fence, jumping from the upper rail to the shingled roof. A few steps and he'd make the window.

He howled his success into the sunset then lowered his body to the window ledge. Balancing, he pressed his nose to the glass, spotting Boo inside.

But she wasn't alone. On the other side of the bars, facing her, stood her mother.

Oh, this couldn't be good.

He pawed the pane. "Meow!"

A net fell around him. "Gotcha!"

CHAPTER

TWELVE

"I'm surprised they're allowing me visitors. Especially the one who put in a false report to get me arrested," Boo spat at her mother, who looked at her from the other side of the bars.

The dismal gray walls of the jail cell sapped the color from Cecilia's face, and the single bulb overhead added to her mother's ghoulish appearance.

Boo quelled a hiss and took a step back, lowering her hands. If she wanted a chance to call Alyce and get all this sorted out, then fighting with her mother wouldn't help.

Still, Boo glared at her mother, whose perfectly ironed white pantsuit looked out of place in the dank surroundings.

"Would it surprise you to know that I'd hoped you'd simply stay out of my town?" Cecilia asked.

The nerve of Mom.

"Willow Wisp doesn't belong to you, Mom, much as you like to think it does," Boo taunted.

Cecilia bared her fangs and snarled.

"Corral your temper, Mother." Her mother's anger

pressed down on Boo as if a tangible force, forcing Boo to gasp to escape suffocation.

Boo removed herself from the confrontation, plopping onto the lumpy cot and running her fingers along the stained mattress on the metal rim.

The threadbare piping indicated an aged mattress. The toilet, which sat in a dark corner, whined, the water continuously filling and draining the bowl simultaneously.

There wasn't a flimsy, paper ass gasket in sight!

Only a thin, metal seatless rim.

Boo hacked.

"You only have yourself to blame," Cecilia said as she evoked a staring contest.

Childish games. Mother dominates the Olympic sport.

When Boo was young, she'd played this game with her mother. Boo recalled how one of them would tire and blink, resulting in a fit of laughter. Back then, they never ridiculed and blamed each other for breaking contact.

But not now. Boo's mother had set out to prove a point, and her grape-sized green eyes bulged to their limits.

Boo knew that resolve like the back of her paw.

Where did her mother's pain originate?

Boo knew hers sprang from Cecilia's rejection and insistence on obedience and perfection.

"What happened to you, Mom? Why are you so angry?" *At me?*

As the sun set, Cecilia lifted her gaze to the small, barred window, her face a mask of bitterness and frustration. "Is my demeanor really that surprising? How else is a mother to react to offspring that turned out so disappointing?"

Her mother's words stung like Boo had fallen into a hornet's nest.

Still, she shoved the hurt down deep. "What are you blaming me for? I've done everything for you."

At least Boo had tried before she'd been jailed that first time. While her mother worked, Boo had taken charge of household duties and meal prep along with her curriculum.

"Everything you've done has dragged our family name through the mud," Cecilia elaborated. "You're reckless. I'd hoped that being jailed once would have been enough. For a time, it seemed that way. Sure, you kept an apartment in town, so I had to keep my eye on your movements, but you never returned to the graveyard. I'd foolishly hoped that you were done with all that."

Boo clenched her balled fists, struggling to keep her composure. She wished she'd kept that Botox appointment she didn't need so that her face wouldn't twitch from frustration.

Her mother was driving her mad.

"Mom, everything I did was to please you. Seeing you angry all the time was hard on me. I didn't know how to fix what others had broken in you."

"I never asked you to take care of me." Cecilia winced. "I was the parent. I was the one responsible for you."

"Responsible for me?" Boo checked more things off the mental list when her mother had failed her.

Abuse.

Neglect.

Abandonment.

That time Cecilia dragged Boo to the ER, convinced she'd seen her husband's ghost.

Boo continued, "How many times did I come home from school hungry and find an empty refrigerator? Then, when you held down a job, I was left to cook dinner for us, do the laundry, clean the house, and keep perfect grades to keep you from seeing spirits. Forgive me if I may have acted like a petulant child, but I had my reasons."

Boo jumped up to a standing position and paced in a tight circle around the dirty drain cover in the center of the room. She had to spring this cell, but how?

The steel bars and block walls allowed her no chance at freedom, but she gripped the bars, attempting to rip them from their foundations like she was as strong as Willy.

Shocker. She wasn't.

Her mother growled. "Look at how capable you are today. Look at how much better you are than me."

"Is that what you think?" Boo had never put words to her reasons for grave robbing. She'd never seen her tasks as something meant to develop character or to outrank her mother. Boo was simply trying to rectify past wrongdoings.

She'd only wanted her mother's approval, but perhaps she only needed her own.

Her mother was incapable of seeing Boo as more than an irritant.

Sure, Boo had wanted to guarantee that the artifacts would be returned to local families, but she couldn't discount the joy she felt when she failed at finding the original owner or descendant.

Boo had celebrated helping her mother grow their museum's collection of artifacts, which fueled Boo's drive to hunt for more items, as each earned a crumb of approval from Cecilia.

Cecilia huffed. "You think you helped me?"

Boo nodded. "The better your museum did, the more money you made, and for once, I didn't go hungry. You seemed content."

"Content?" Cecilia exclaimed. "Because of you, I'm forever branded the mother of a criminal."

Boo sat quietly, picking at a string at the corner of the mattress, pondering her arrest years before. "If you hadn't called the police, I wouldn't have been charged with a crime."

Cecilia clucked her tongue. "So, you've branded yourself a hero? You and your gorilla?"

"Willy is a chimera, Mother. And don't bring him into this." Boo took a deep, shuddering breath.

Mercifully, Cecilia listened for once.

The subsequent silence was amplified by the whining toilet, and someone rattled their cage in the distance.

Boo didn't know how long she'd be stuck in the holding cell. The phantom taste of bland food and day-old bread of the prison cafeteria rode her tastebuds. The flip-flops she'd worn the last time she was incarcerated had never fit her feet, and she'd occasionally rolled her ankles. That was bound to happen again.

Boo ripped the thread and tossed it onto the concrete floor, overwhelmed by the enormity of her situation.

Drip, drip, drip.

Her mother sniffed, and she rubbed her eyes.

Was she crying?

Cecilia was giving Boo whiplash with her emotions, and Boo struggled to know how to read the woman.

Heartless Cecilia never once showed her sadness, not since that time she'd landed in the ER, years and years ago.

The closer Boo studied her mother, the more she wondered if her mother's sadness encompassed more than her disappointment.

When Boo met her mother's gaze, her eyes were red-rimmed and beginning to swell.

"You can stop the show, Mother. I'm not one of your constituents."

"Is that what you think of me?" Cecilia's voice hitched. "That I'm an ice queen?"

Boo glanced at her hands, wishing she had her knife to comfort her.

Cecilia admitted, "I didn't want you to suffer the same fate as your father."

Boo sucked a breath. Had she heard her mom correctly? "What fate did Dad suffer?"

"You weren't much more than three years old the night your father disappeared," Cecilia explained. "He learned of a secret from a man he met in the cemetery."

Scooting closer to the edge of her cot, Boo narrowed her gaze at her mom. "What man?"

"I never met him, but he claimed there were riches beneath the cemetery." Cecilia unbuttoned the top button of her suit. "We were struggling, Thom and me. It was a bad time for our kind. Then you came along."

A bad time for our kind? Oh, yes, the feline leukemia virus, FeLV, combined with the threat of cat-scratch fever. Yowl!

A disease and bacterial infection Boo had no control over, just like she had no control over how her mother perceived her or treated her.

"Stop blaming me. Maybe you should have thought twice before bringing me into the world." As Boo said the words, she shuddered, and the rickety bed rattled.

Cecilia picked at her cuticle and then brushed her eyes with the heels of her hands. "Anyway, your father went into the cemetery with this man to learn the truth about what lay below the grass, and he never returned."

"Are you going to talk nonsense about some portal, like Ginnie?" Boo asked with an exasperated sigh.

"It's not nonsense; it's the truth."

Boo shook her head and rolled her eyes. "Okay, and this portal caused my father to disappear?"

Cecilia nodded, her eyes glistening with unshed tears. "I suspect, like you, he was curious, but in his case, curiosity killed the cat. Thom's desire to prove the existence of other worlds was lost in the void. I've tried to cover it up, to keep you safe and to protect you from your curiosity. I couldn't have you following in his footsteps."

"And you'd rather see me jailed than dead. You'd rather treat me like you didn't love me, so I'd stay away from you and, thereby, Willow Wisp. So I'd stay *above* the lawn."

Her mother's eyes rained, and her chest pumped as she ugly cried.

Was this the miracle Boo had waited for?

"All of it's true," Cecilia admitted. "The police gave up when no one bothered the headstones. The cemetery has been quiet for four years until last night. I made you the villain in the cover-up, and I'm so sorry. I never stopped loving you. I'm so proud of who you've become as a woman."

Proud? Loved her?

Boo hated crying. She never thought she'd be a dripping mess in her mother's presence, but Boo understood sacrificing for those she loved. So had her mother.

Boo sprang from her cot and ran to the bars, tossing her arms around her mother's thin shoulders to hug her despite the barrier between them.

The woman stiffened briefly before melting against Boo.

"I'm so sorry, Boo. I thought if I pushed you away, you'd stay safe." Cecilia inched back, meeting Boo's teary gaze.

"I guess we're both guilty of our screw-ups." Boo pushed back from her mother, dusting off the crusted dirt on her jeans and noticing that soil had fallen on her mother's white outfit.

"Sorry. I've got my dirt on you." Boo brushed off her mom's pants.

Cecilia stilled Boo's hands. "This outfit is as much a front as my lies. It's about time I get dirty again."

This turn of events was more than Boo could have asked for. "Well, we have a chance to fix our mess, and I have an idea."

Her mother had answered all the questions that had run through Boo's mind since Boo's original incarceration. They had one more day to pull together until it was summer solstice, and it was already early Friday morning. "Guard!"

The stocky woman marched toward the cell, giving Boo a stern look. "Problem?"

"No problem," Cecilia piped up. "I'm dropping the charges. It turns out, I was mistaken about my daughter."

Mom looked at Boo with love in her eyes, something Boo had wished for her whole life.

"I'll see what I can do." The guard narrowed her brown gaze before strolling down the corridor and disappearing behind a locked door.

"She looks thrilled with her job," Boo said, stepping back from the bars.

Cecilia held Boo's shoulders. "Don't worry. I'm sure my lawyer is already on his way."

No sooner had her mother said the words than a man appeared, his suit as crisp as if he'd been dunked in Faultless starch.

"Stan Freedom, this is Boo Bombay, my daughter. Boo, this is Stan." Cecilia gestured between Boo and the lawyer.

"Ms. Bombay." Stan nodded. "I've heard many good things about you over the years."

Good things?

"I'm dropping the charges," Cecilia reiterated. "I'm sorry for the paperwork that might cause, but I made a mistake. One I need you to help me rectify."

"Oh." The lawyer pursed his lips and then nodded, likely happy to charge Cecilia for the extra work.

The guard returned, unlocking the cell, allowing Boo to exit and follow the group down to the processing desk.

As Stan and the officer worked on the paperwork, Cecilia glanced at her daughter. "So, why did you return to town?"

"I have tickets to the auction at the museum tonight," Boo offered. "I'm... well, I'm on assignment. Supposedly, someone there owns a heart-shaped stone that belongs to the Bastet statue."

"You're on an assignment?"

Boo nodded. "I'm working for the Furry United Coalition. I'm officially a cadet, but the director is allowing me and Willy to—"

Her words were cut off when her mother pulled her into a tight hug.

"I've never felt prouder of you," Cecilia stated. "My daughter, working for FUC! You should be very proud of yourself."

When Cecilia finally let her go and Boo caught her breath, she realized that if Mom knew about FUC, she'd know about Alyce. Boo added, "I wish Alyce would have spelled out what this stone looks like."

"I think I may have a clue," Cecilia said. "I know about the Bastet statue. The stone is a zebra heart—a black and white jasper stone. The gem has powers, including cell regeneration. It's a powerful protection stone, warding off negative energy and helping to keep the owner safe from harm."

"Miss Bombay, you're free to go," the officer announced, holding out a plastic bag containing her belongings.

The contents included shoes, a cell phone, ID, an ornate-handled knife, and the necklace she'd found years ago: a gold necklace with a heart-shaped, black and white stone.

CHAPTER

THIRTEEN

Back behind the women's side of the jail, Willy fought against the net that held him. His captor made haste toward the men's side of the jail while Willy jostled in her net, his paws and tail sticking through the mesh.

He scratched at the mesh. "Yowl!"

"Animal Control is looking for you," the woman said with a *shush*.

Willy swatted at her legs and pressed his whiskers through the mesh, begging for freedom. "*YOWL!*"

"Hold on a little longer." The woman upped her pace, her heels *click-clacking* on the outside walkway that wrapped the buildings.

Where was she taking him? Back to jail?

The growl he emitted next caused her to finally stop and hold the bag up to face level. "Cadet Tagger, that's enough. I'm Suzie Khue, a FUC plant here at the police agency. Had you stayed in your cell a bit longer, I would have gotten you out. What's more, you would have been released, regardless, because the charges have been dropped."

129

Did he hear her right? "Meow?"

"I'd be confused, too, but play along until I get things figured out and ditch that mean, menacing Officer Merl Rotty." Suzie removed him from the net and tossed it under the bushes fronting the station.

Willy squirmed in her arms, pushing against the woman who tried to tuck his sleek, black body under her sweater as if she *could* hide a twenty-five-pound Bombay.

She gripped him by his nape, and his legs dangled midair. "Hold still. You're not making hiding you easy."

It wasn't like Willy *could* shift back into his human form with law enforcement deputies marching between the parking lot and the station and Officer Rotty looking for him. Not to mention, he'd ditched all his clothing and frowned at tacking on an indecent exposure charge.

He was in enough trouble as it was.

As soon as he found a private place and regained his human form, he'd place a call to Alyce—

A man dressed in a white coverall stalked toward them. "Let me give you a hand with that mangy stray."

Mangy?

Before Suzie could protest, the animal control officer gripped Willy with gloved hands and heaved Willy into the air, inspecting the space under his tail.

"It's a stray tomcat in desperate need of neutering. Look at the size of those—"

"Yowl!" Willy twisted, and his body shook. Things were going from bad to worse, and he had flashbacks of evil DIC.

"You found my bad, bad boy!"

Boo?

Willy's heart warmed, and his stress melted at the sound of Boo's voice.

The love of his life pulled him into her arms. She snuggled her face against his shoulder. "I missed you so much!"

She smelled like spring sunshine, after-shower rainbows, and the kind of happiness that brought tears to his eyes.

Damn, his love for Boo was downright magical. His world was perfectly rosy if she held him and told him she'd never leave his side.

"I've been looking all over for you," Boo purred. "I take my eyes off you for one minute, and you wind up frazzled, but I'm here now. I'm not going anywhere."

The story was a flat-out lie. Well, most of it. Not the frazzled part.

Suzie looked choked up as she brushed her cheeks.

The officer rubbed his chin and rolled his eyes as if he could see right through Boo's BS.

Willy nuzzled Boo. "*Meow, meow, meow, meow. Meow, meow, meow, meow. Meow, meow, meow, meow. Meow, meow, meow, meow.*"

Damn, he meant every word.

He loved Boo with all his heart. She was his *home*.

"As you can see, my baby isn't a stray at all, and I'll square everything away with licensing as soon as we're finished here." Boo batted her eyelashes. "We *are* finished, aren't we, Officer Rotty?"

They'd put their love for each other on display, which not even the officer could deny.

Merl cleared his throat and tucked a card into Boo's hand. "Information regarding neutering, vaccinations, and licensing is on the back."

Boo touched Merl on the sleeve. "Will do, officer. I appreciate your concern. Willow Wisp can't have wild animals breeding uncontrolled and upping the populations of unwanted pets."

Satisfied, Merl waddled away, hitching up his coveralls as he went.

Willy let out the breath he'd been holding. *Whew, that was a close one.*

"It's your lucky day, Cadet Tagger." Suzie patted Willy's head. "Looks like both of you have another life, another day. Try not to find yourselves jailed again any time soon."

After thanking Suzie, Boo sighed. "That was a close call. Luckily, my mother dropped her charges against both of us."

Cecilia to the rescue? What were the odds?

"Let's find a place for you to shift," Boo said. "I have your clothes and a plan."

The public restroom located in the park centered in town, a block from the police station, gave Willy the hiding spot he needed to shift and dress.

More importantly, upon exiting the restroom, he set his lips on Boo's and kissed her like he hadn't seen her in a decade. "I love you."

"I know," she purred.

He wrapped her in a hug. "And thank you for rescuing me before that monster cut off my balls."

"You're welcome." Boo held his hand, and they walked back to the police station, where their vehicles were waiting. Boo had the keys for both, and she handed his over.

"We should probably check in with Alyce," Willy remarked. "I'm sure she's tracking us and is aware that we never made it to the Bluetique."

"I talked to her right after we were released. She knows what happened."

"All right." He fiddled with his van keys. "Where to?"

"I want to see if we can talk to Zeb. I'm certain he knows way more than he's letting on."

Willy scratched his head. Could everyone have an important part in this mission? He asked, "In what way?"

She looked hesitant to explain. Finally, she said, "My mother backs Ginnie's story about a portal beneath the town. My mother says the portal took my father."

"That makes no sense." Willy looked at her doubtfully. "Are you really believing any of that?"

"I don't know. But I do think that everything is coded. Zeb Earhart is an anagram for Zebra Heart, which is this stone we're supposed to track down." She pulled the necklaces out from under her shirt. "And I've had the key all along."

"Are you sure that's the one?"

Boo nodded, and her eyes watered. "You'll think me morbid, but I dug up my father's gravesite back when I was, you know... After finding other graves empty, I just had a feeling about his, and sure enough, it was empty... except for this necklace."

"That's a strange coincidence."

"Is it though?" she asked, tilting her head. "I believe the Bastet statue belongs to my family, and if the stone belongs to the statue, then maybe my father had located it and held it until he could find the statue. Or maybe the stone had stayed in our family, even after the statue was stolen."

"That's why you know so much about the statue..." Willy started piecing the picture together.

"Yes," she admitted. "I'd even toyed with the idea of stealing the statue for myself. Honestly, I'm glad someone else stole it first, because things turned out better this way."

"Boo!" Willy shook his head in disbelief. "After all this

time, giving up a life of crime and almost becoming a FUC agent, and you would have given it all up for some statue?"

"I had the misguided thought that if I had it and gave it to my mother then maybe that would finally be the thing to reconnect us."

"It's not like she could have displayed it in her museum! Not a stolen artifact!"

She nodded. "I figured it would stay in the family vault."

"Why?"

"Look, I know now it's a bunch of folklore and legend, but all that talk Ginnie was doing about a portal and such? She's retelling my family history. We're protectors, keeping our homes safe from whatever threats exist, and centuries ago the Bastet statue was among the items we kept safe. Or, rather, we kept the world safe *from*."

Willy took a deep breath, glad that the statue was locked away in Alyce's vault and that Boo's misguided plan had not come to fruition. "You are a more effective protector when you're working for FUC."

"I know." She hung her head.

"Well, what's done is done. Now, do you want to tell me why your mother dropped the charges?"

"We made some sort of breakthrough, I guess. We'll see how it goes, but for the moment, there is a truce."

"Okay." Then, Willy remembered something he'd yet to share with her. "Tal Basta isn't a person. It's a location in Cairo, which I believe are the coordinates Zeb, or whatever his real name is, whispered to you. Tal Basta is a Bastet temple."

Boo's green eyes widened, and her mouth fell open for a moment. She removed the necklace and tucked it into her pocket. "It's all coming together, but what are you thinking?"

Willy's mind crowded with scenarios, leading to one clear thought. "I'm thinking we need to talk to Zeb."

Boo reached for Willy, taking his offered hand and lacing their fingers. "This necklace is sentimental to me. I don't want to give it up, to put it with the statue to be held in some museum when it's... well, when I feel like it's rightfully *mine*."

"Let's talk to Alyce, see what she says." Willy had enough experience with the woman that he knew Alyce would hear them out.

Boo nodded. "Maybe. I'll take my own car and meet you there, okay? I want to run by my apartment and change first."

Locked inside the grimy jail, Willy understood wanting to redress. "Sure thing."

Willy drove to the Academy, his foot depressed against the gas pedal until he cruised through the gates and parked.

He paused just outside the WANC entrance. Both students and staff filtered in and out of the doors, as nocturnal shifters—owls, bats, foxes, raccoons, opossums, skunks, etcetera—attended their classes.

He continued until he reached the director's office, which was empty. Her assistant, Eliza, wasn't at her desk, and Alyce wasn't at hers, either, though both doors were open. He figured that meant they'd be back soon, so he entered, taking a seat across from Alyce's desk.

His eyes were drawn to the closet.

Suddenly, he was standing, striding over to the closet as though someone used him like a living puppet. All other thoughts left him as his body and mind were overtaken by the overpowering urge to see the statue...

To touch it.

His heart jack-rabbited in his chest as he opened the closet, spotting the safe.

Willy checked the safe, finding it locked. There was no surprise there. But that didn't stop his efforts. His hand moved automatically, punching in a guess at a code—a code that didn't open the safe.

But that didn't stop him. He was strong.

More robust than a silverback.

Chimera strong, and possessing the ability to morph his body into a King Kong beast.

Willy gritted through the shift, his bones elongating and his muscles bulking to perfection.

He wrapped his arms around the safe and squeezed.

Pressure built behind his eyeballs, and his muscles shook as he strained to break the safe.

He wasn't sure where his power came from. Perhaps it was his altered DNA or his adrenaline kicking in, like when a father saves his child by lifting a car.

The hinges snapped, and the door lock crumbled.

He wasn't a father, though perhaps one day Boo would bless him with a child, so he couldn't attribute his strength to love.

But something drove him to connect with the statue. Something he couldn't explain.

As he stared at his monstrous reflection in the destroyed safe, he sucked in a breath.

The golden phallus-shaped Bastet statue with the hole for the missing stone shimmered.

Electricity seemed to skitter across his skin, and the lavender aura mesmerized him.

The artifact called to him, begged him to covet it, to follow the energy that left him mindless and singular in his desires.

Forget the mission.

Forget Boo.

Forget the innocent lives threatened by the powerful artifact.

You're the Chosen One.

Willy reached for the statue that spoke to him.

The euphoric waves that rushed over him were better than bananas foster and sex.

"Willy, don't let the magic steal your mind."

Boo's voice filtered through the magic.

"Willy, I'd die all over again if I lost you."

Her voice grew stronger, louder, reaching the center of his brain.

"Willy, look away. Come back to me."

The touch on his shoulder barely registered.

When he glanced across, thinking Boo was standing beside him, it was an illusion.

He'd only been inside Alyce's office a few minutes, but he gasped as he spotted the artifact in his clutches. The floor beneath him seemed to spiral like he was about to fall into a time portal.

He blinked, trying to erase the threat.

He wasn't a monster.

He wasn't covetous.

Willy deposited the statue on Alyce's desk, and the strange mind trick that had encapsulated him faded away.

What was that? He didn't know, but what he was certain of? The statue wanted him to take it back to the Willow Wisp cemetery.

He had to do it. There was no other choice.

But he could at least take some precautions.

Willy found the gloves Alyce had used in her desk drawer. He squeezed his hands into them, grabbed the statue, and bolted from the building, toward Boo, toward their happy future.

CHAPTER

FOURTEEN

Boo arrived back at her apartment and had just stepped inside when her phone rang. She didn't recognize the number but answered anyway.

"So, Alyce tells me you've been on quite the adventure," Zeb said, his voice as sharp as ever.

Boo's heart squeezed from relief. "Zeb! I'm so glad you're okay!"

"I heard you brought Alyce the statue."

"I did..." Boo answered slowly, unsure whether the reason he was calling was to thank her for a job well done or if he had other reasons. She had so many questions to ask him but couldn't figure out what to ask first.

"You impress me, Cadet Bombay. After our first meeting, I was certain that you had nefarious intentions, but you've proven me wrong. Good job."

"Uh, thanks." She didn't feel she needed to assure him that his instincts had been correct. "Hey, uh, I was wondering, have you heard anything about a portal under the city of Willow Wisp?"

Zeb was silent for a moment. "Portals are a thing of fantasy, and we live in a world of science."

"That didn't answer my question," Boo aptly assessed.

"Have I heard people make the claim? Sure," he admitted. "But does such a thing exist? Of course not."

"Right." What had she expected a well-respected FUC agent to say? Knowing she'd already sounded foolish, she decided to go all in. "Zeb, what do you know about the missing stone? Have you ever seen it? You didn't... uh, bury it in an empty grave or anything, did you?"

"I've never seen the stone, no. If I had, don't you think I would have reunited it with the statue?"

"Right," she said again, disappointed that her conversation with Zeb wasn't more enlightening. Or perhaps she was simply dejected that the fantasy story her mother had concocted wasn't true.

"In any case, good work, future Agent Bombay."

With that, he hung up.

She thought over the conversation as she showered and changed into clean clothes. It felt good to wash away the stench of jail, but she wished she would have gotten more out of Zeb. It seemed like everything that had happened with Ginnie and her mother had made her think that there was more to Zeb's involvement with the statue and the history of Willow Wisp than really existed.

After she made herself a quick meal and finished it, her cell buzzed again. She checked the screen, thinking maybe it was Zeb calling back, ready to amend his statements, but it wasn't.

It was Willy.

Her heart warmed, and her belly fluttered. "Hey."

"Where are you?" Willy asked, an alarming *whoo-oo-whoo-oo-whoo* coming through the receiver.

"I'm at my apartment." Boo pressed her ear to the cell, trying to make out the background noises. "Where are *you?*"

"In town." Willy panted. "The Willow Wisp town emergency alarm is going off. I heard someone say there's a gas leak."

Strange. Her apartment building wasn't far from downtown, but she didn't hear any alarms.

Willy continued, "Only, I don't smell natural gas. You know, that rotten egg smell. Cops are mostly congregated in and around the cemetery."

"The *cemetery?*" *The portal.* Yes, Zeb said it was fantasy, and her rational mind agreed, but her gut instinct told her there was something to it. "We have to go check it out."

Then a thought occurred to her. "Willy, why are you in town? I thought we were meeting at the Academy to give Alyce the necklace to go with the statue?"

"I did go to the Academy, but then I came back."

"Okay... why?"

"Because I stole the statue."

"*What?*" For a moment, Boo thought maybe she was dreaming the phone conversation. "That doesn't make any sense!"

"I know it sounds strange, but I went to Alyce's office, and the statue called out to me."

Boo's heart sank. Legend of the statue claimed it was dangerous, and while she never believed it—until Zeb had been poisoned—Willy's words shook her.

She urged, "You have to take it back to the Academy."

Instead of listening to her, Willy stated, "Meet me at the cemetery. You'll have to use back streets and alleys to get to the mausoleum."

Knowing she couldn't reason with him over the phone, she said, "I'll be there as soon as I can."

She ended the call and pocketed her cell.

What was going on? A gas leak in the cemetery and Willy following orders from a statue? One thing was for sure; Boo was going to do whatever it took to save her man.

She left her apartment, jumping into her car, and speeding across town. She parked a few blocks away from the cemetery to avoid the road closures around the center of town.

As Willy had described, red and blue lights strobed against the skyline, and police officers patrolled the blockades. Sirens sent echoes through the streets.

Talk about a shitshow.

Boo exited the car and sent a text to Willy, but he didn't answer back.

Her chest squeezed from fear that she'd rekindled her love for Willy and that flame could be snuffed out if the statue led him into harm's way.

Ping.

Boo glanced down, spotting the time and Willy's text: *Wait for me near the mausoleum.*

He didn't say when he'd be there, but she trusted Willy to follow through.

She flipped up her hoodie, and mindful of the cops patrolling the streets, her cat burglar skills kicked in, using the familiarity she had with the town alleyways and the underground storm drain system.

She opened a utility hole cover, shoving back the heavy metal disk before entering.

Sticky cobwebs tangled her legs, and a putrid smell of rotting leaves hit her nose.

She descended a crusty ladder, praying it wouldn't spring from its rusty hinges.

How old was this infrastructure? Why wasn't the town prioritizing the conditions below the city?

Ten rungs later, she landed on the bottom of an eight-foot diameter concrete culvert beneath the town. She figured she was three blocks from Main Street, and four blocks from Willow Wisp Way, the cemetery's southwest corner cross street.

Her head swam. She flicked on her cell phone, lighting up the soupy path.

Overhead, the light from the streetlamps made its way through the drains, somewhat illuminating the sewer, and Boo pocketed her cell to save power.

The voices of law enforcement officers reached into the drainage system, echoing in the tubular space. "Keep the perimeter. There is a gas leak in the cemetery."

She stopped, looking up to find a utility hole, knowing that if she went much farther, she'd end up at the river.

The wobbly metal ladder shook in its welds, but Boo kept her faith.

It *would* hold.

She *would* meet up with Willy.

She *would* save him before the statue led him to his demise.

She popped her head out of the hole and took in her surroundings. She was at street level and positioned along the interior road that ran through the cemetery.

She purred, a calming hum. "Things are going our way."

Inside her pocket, she reached past her blade and clutched her necklace, noticing the slightest static prick in her palm.

The mausoleum was up ahead. She could make out the

rosebushes flanking the stone sides and the marble cherub over the double doors. She headed toward it, skirting a giant pine, weaving her way between the monuments of the founding families, and then stopped twenty feet from the stone structure.

"Willy?" she whisper-shouted.

Her heart flooded with relief when he revealed himself.

His torso was bare, and his abs shimmered in the moonlight.

Talk about a god.

Willy held the bundled statue.

Boo sprinted toward Willy and sailed into his arms, knowing he'd catch her every time.

Static stormed between them as they sandwiched the artifact. It was powerful, but so was their love for each other. "I missed you. I'm so glad you're okay."

Willy kissed Boo. "For a few moments back at the Academy, I was overcome. I don't know why, but it was like I lost control and just *had* to get the statue and bring it back here."

"We should call Alyce. We need to get it back to her." Yet, even as the words left her mouth, she knew that wasn't going to happen.

"Are you thinking what I'm thinking?" Willy asked.

"That the statue and necklace want to be here and be reunited." It was strange, feeling like two inanimate objects had desires, but she knew to her core that there was no other way.

Boo shoved her hand into her pocket and locked her fingers around the necklace. She didn't want to let it go but accepted some things were bigger than her.

Willy drew Boo's hand from her pocket, telling her, "I know this necklace means a lot to you because you believe your dad left it for you. He'd be so proud of you if he saw how brave and compassionate you've become."

She nodded, accepting her goodness. Before, she'd been self-critical and disappointed in her decisions. But no longer. She saw herself differently, her image one of positivity and self-acceptance.

A leader.

With that thought, she said, "Let's go."

"Where?"

Boo didn't answer. She just trotted ahead, knowing Willy would follow. She followed her inner compass, while her booming pulse pounded in her ears.

She halted at Thom Bombay's headstone.

Boo's heart rolled. It seemed her heart was doing a lot of somersaults as a surprise certainty took hold. "The portal is below my father's fake resting place."

"It's where you found the necklace, right?" Willy motioned to her hand.

"If there is a portal, and I enter it, do you think I'd find my dad?"

Willy's expression turned hard. "You're not seriously thinking that's possible, are you?"

Boo shook her head regretfully. "No, but it's kind of nice to think something like that could be possible."

"This is messed up," Willy said, taking a step away from the grave.

"What's wrong?" Boo asked. "You're the one who brought the statue here!"

Though she'd been the one to go along with it, spurred on by some mysterious urge inside of her to do it.

"What are we doing?" Willy grappled with the statue. "We have two artifacts that FUC wants, and we're going to, what? Just bury them here? Or are we supposed to dig and dig and dig until we find some supposed portal?"

"I don't know," she admitted, popping the stone from its platinum setting and pocketing the empty pendant and chain.

A gloved Willy placed the stone into the divot under the statue cat's chin, and the lavender aura lit up, more brightly than ever. Bright enough to illuminate the cemetery. He placed the renewed artifact on her father's monument, snapping it into the flower holder. "Stand back!"

Boo slid her feet backward, her nerves causing her to pant. Was she doing the right thing?

Hackles rose as the ground quaked. The wind whirled, howling through the trees, and her hair stood on end.

A murder of crows cawed above, their wings beating as they rode the cyclone.

Willy slid his hand into hers, the two fusing their excitement and fear as the grass at their feet faded.

An aurora borealis exploded from her father's grave, sending Boo reeling as the atmosphere thundered.

Willy yelled, "Get back!"

Boo shouted, "Willy, run!"

They spun but froze in place when faced with a man holding a gun.

FIFTEEN

Willy couldn't believe how this night was playing out. Willow Wisp's mayor, Richard Joystick, gripped a pistol in one hand and held Cecilia Bombay by the neck with the other. Her green eyes reflected the aurora's starburst of colors, which had risen to the heavens. The poor woman's legs trembled as if her knees were about to give out. But that half-inch barrel pointed at Willy looked the size of a cannon.

"Get away from my mom!" Boo shouted. She gripped Willy's arm. "We have to do something."

Willy projected his voice. "Put the gun down, Mayor Joystick. Reuniting the statue and stone doesn't have to end in anyone getting killed. Let's talk this out."

Richard dragged Cecilia through the grass, weaving around the array of headstones as if dancing in Stonehenge. "The time for talking is over. I'm minutes away from owning the key to a portal that can take me anywhere I want to go."

The words sounded like the ramblings of a madman. Richard had been mayor for years. Willy had never known another mayor since his birth. And no one had ever suggested that Richard was out of his mind.

Willy recalled the effect the statue had on him earlier in Alyce's office. Is that what was happening to Richard? He reasoned that if he was able to snap out of it—to some degree, though it was debatable, considering he'd still taken the statue from FUCN'A and brought it to the cemetery—it could be possible to talk Richard down. "You don't want to do this."

"You know nothing of what I want. Now, hand it over, or else." The mayor clucked his tongue and pointed the business end of the wooden-handled pistol to Cecilia's temple.

"No!" Boo cried, and her face paled.

"Don't do it," Cecilia shouted. "If Richard gets his way, he may rewrite history."

Richard shook the woman. "Shut your mouse trap, Cecilia. You've been lying to all of us, telling me you didn't know where the stone had disappeared to when your daughter had it all along."

The fiery aurora continued burning up the heavens. Willy shielded his eyes from the blinding light. It was doubtful he could shift and pounce on Richard now without risking Cecilia.

"You're right," Cecilia shouted. "I had it, and I buried it where I knew Boo would find it. She's a smart girl like her father. I knew she'd eventually put together the puzzle pieces because she's the best daughter a mother could have. I admire you, Boo."

Willy dared a glance at Boo and spotted the emotion gathering in her eyes. The bittersweet moment shoved Willy into protective mode. He would save Cecilia and reunite mother and daughter if that was the last thing he did.

"I said shut it, Cecilia." Mayor Joystick locked his grip and pulled Cecilia closer to the glowing statue and the gaping hole that continued to grow in front of Thom Bombay's tombstone. Pieces of earth spilled from the edges, filling a seemingly never-ending hole. From where the mayor held Cecilia, he couldn't reach over the pit to grab the artifact.

Willy winced when a significant portion of the lawn fell into the hole. "Stand down. Please."

Richard skirted the opening, trying his best to reach the object. "Retrieve the statue, and hand it over."

Willy padded forward, his toes connected to the network of roots below the earth, the energy of the moment sparking something inside of him. With every passing minute, he felt his chimerism narrowing to something more than he'd been. Something he needed to become to save the woman he loved and her mother.

And it scared the hell out of him.

Willy asked, "What is it you really want, Mayor?"

"Money may be the root of all evil, but I'll never be wealthy and powerful enough. I'm tired of being mayor. I want to rule the night."

Darkness? From history, Willy pictured rulers like Genghis Khan and Vlad the Impaler.

Willy's hair stood on end at the idea of the mayor ruling. He'd seen madmen in charge, like DIC, that horrible power-obsessed doctor who'd stripped Willy of his silver-back DNA and replaced it with a menagerie.

Willy took another step forward, inching closer to the mayor. If he could convince the mayor to let go of Cecilia, he might have a chance at disarming him. "How about a trade? Cecilia for me?"

"No, Willy," both Cecilia and Boo said in unison.

Boo begged, "Willy, please. There must be another bargaining chip."

Willy dared a glance at Boo. Her big green eyes held a pleading look.

What were his options? He had to believe in himself. "Trust me. I have a plan."

Willy didn't have time to think it through, but he had to take the chance to resolve the situation. Boo gave him a subtle nod as if telling him she believed in him doing the right thing.

Blind faith.

The ground cracked underfoot, and the sod split under Willy's feet.

He hopped, trying to reclaim his balance, any landing a poor option.

If he fell toward the mayor and the portal, he could potentially save Cecilia, but it yielded an uncertain future if he should fail at saving her.

If he stepped backward toward Boo, which gave him no chance of saving Cecilia, Boo would forever be heartbroken without the mother she'd just reconciled with.

"I believe in you, Willy. I believe in us forever." Boo's eyes watered. "Love is worth sacrificing for."

Did she want him to stay with her or for him to take out the villain?

The ground rocked violently. It could have been nine on the Richter scale.

Boo sprang toward her mom, but Willy leaped, the two colliding. Boo fell to the side.

Bang!

The gun fired, and a bullet whizzed past Willy's ear.

Cecilia shifted into her feline form and disappeared from the mayor's grasp.

Before Richard got off a second shot, Willy launched himself and tackled the man, sending him to the ground.

Grrrr. Willy pinned Richard's weaponed hand. "It's over, Mayor."

"Over? The fight has just started." Richard hissed, and his body shrank under Willy, lengthening. His skin mottled, turning a dark yellow with purple dots that lined both sides of his slithering form.

WTF is happening?

Was Mayor Richard a closet shifter?

The more Willy scrutinized the shifter, the more he realized that the man was more like him, not precisely a complete snake shifter but some form of chimera.

Willy tightened his grip on the mayor's torso, but the man thinned further, and the weapon landed on the ground.

Willy kicked the pistol and watched it disappear into the shadows.

The mayor slid free of his trousers, and his legs fused.

Willy shuffled backward, trying to get a better grip on the man, but the mayor's sidewinding, serpentine thrusts hindered Willy's hold.

"What are you?" Willy demanded.

Richard's forked tongue jabbed at the air as he rose. "It's not *what* I am, but *who* I am."

"Well, you want to fill me in?" Willy's mind spun. The aurora lit up the sky, casting strange shadows, and he swore that they slithered over the headstones.

Slithered?

"Snakes!" Boo kicked, and a snake flew past Willy, its body gyrating like a wonky boomerang.

More snakes crawled toward them, at least a dozen hissing asps striking the air.

"Stop this madness, Mayor!" Cecilia called out from her perch on an overhanging branch.

Even if Cecilia rejoined the fight, they would still be outnumbered, as the number of vipers mounted.

Unless Willy shifted into his chimera form and unleashed his beast.

Willy wasn't *only* a feline shifter. He was unique, altered, and he'd never pushed his DNA to the limits. He'd come close when he'd broken the safe to retrieve the statue, but he'd controlled his hulkish form.

Now, Willy scratched his head, remembering his history classes and collecting clues about the existence of a snake god named Apep who sought to destroy the sun god. Bastet, a feline shifter, was rumored to have killed Apep with her knife.

If Willy could convince his legs to move, they'd have a chance at defeating the mayor.

The circling snakes stood on their tails, slithering and gaining speed, narrowing their striking distance.

Now or never.

Willy allowed his chimerism to take over, trusting that his body would morph into a shield that could defend against snake bites.

Feathers of steel took over his epidermis. Before his avian mutations swallowed his voice, he gave the order. "Save Willow Wisp! Destroy that statue."

"I've got your back, Willy Tagger!"

Alyce?

Fuck'n A. Alyce was there with backup, the llama shifter looking fierce in her black leathers as she led the FUC agents, and Willy counted a baker's dozen. Even Professor Condor participated, swooping down from the sky and piercing the snakes with his powerful talons.

A double Fuck'n A, Monster Johnson was leading another five Special Ops agents.

The powerful teams targeted the snakes, which emitted a cloying musk scent. A rhumba of rattlesnakes slithered out from the rocky outcroppings dotting the cemetery.

Suzie had shown up, too. Her team of ten members formed a solid perimeter around the cemetery to keep humans from witnessing the shifter extravaganza.

Willy recognized locals, including Ginnie, who'd joined Suzie in de-escalating the frenzy from the on-lookers.

Merl?

Officer Rotty wielded his net, swooping up one asp after another and depositing their writhing forms into a gunnysack. "Water snakes. The tunnels under the city are crawling with these. Might be time for a little flame-throwing barbecue down there."

Willy gulped, and then a piercing blow to his back knocked him to the ground. The unexpected stab cut through bone and reached his lungs. He struggled to breathe, gasping. "*Gr-Gr-Gr-Gr-Gr Gr-Gr!*"

"I am a backstabbing serpent. Nothing I haven't heard before." Richard hissed and exposed his bloodied fangs.

Rolling onto his back, Willy self-healed as best he could and bit back the pain. His chimerism, and that mad DIC, had saved his life, giving him unheard-of healing abilities.

Willy stared at the mayor. This man was out for blood.

In the serpent's eyes, Willy caught a glimpse of his form. He was as bulky as a silverback, his feathered coat as smooth and iridescent as a falcon, but more shocking was his head, somewhere between a horned oryx and a lion.

Willy gulped. He was superb, threatening, and those tiny wings that had been nothing more than an afterthought gave him the ability to fly. No. To soar.

But, without working arms and hands, he was powerless to grab Apep as he stood over him.

Willy panted on the ground, needing time he didn't have to heal fully.

"Willy!" Boo called out.

"You can't save the queen now, beast." Richard struck out at Boo, his serpent speed as fast as the lightning that suddenly struck the aurora.

"No." Willy ignored his pain and punched upright.

Richard constricted his body around Boo's neck and backed her toward the open grave by working his muscular tail.

Willy morphed his fanged mouth enough to plead breathily, "Let her go."

"She's my lucky charm. If I have her, I have the power." Richard—Apep—dragged Boo closer to the flickering aurora and the open grave.

DIC had overpowered Willy, but Willy had helped to send him behind bars for eternity.

If Willy was involved, he'd never let anyone control him again or hurt an innocent for their heinous proposes.

Willy sprouted long cylindrical horns, and his feet sprouted talons. He bobbed and weaved, using his fighting skills to fling asps and rattlers and to keep Apep off balance as the FUC team backed him up, taking out the mounting nests of the snakes.

Boo screamed, "Now!"

He hadn't seen her knife, which she always kept close at hand. The one she nervously clicked in her pocket that day he'd first seen her in the auditorium. Both the necklace and that blade made her feel safe.

She fought to stay with him just as much as he fought for her.

She stabbed her knife into the snake's throat, and the Mayor's hold on his shift wavered.

Willy pushed out hands at the tips of his wings, and his mouth turned to keratin, giving him a beak that could tear off pieces of Apep's flesh.

Boo continued to stab the snake as she clawed at his scales, slicing his flesh until she broke free.

Willy had only a moment of relief over Boo's escape before the ground shook and headstones began to topple.

In human form, Apep twisted and thrashed on the ground. His blood stained the lawn, but still, he reached for the statue with his forked tongue.

"It's mine. I need the power," Apep gurgled.

"Never, Apep!" Willy shouted.

In cat form, Cecilia leaped from a branch and sank her teeth into the mayor's neck.

"You don't taste like chicken." She yacked and spit. Then bit again. "It's time for you to resign as mayor of Willow Wisp!"

Hissssss.

Cecilia dug her claws deeper.

Richard proclaimed, "You'll never break me."

Boo appeared alongside Willy, the two sharing a look before pouncing on Apep and knocking Cecilia to safety.

Willy pummeled Apep and tore at his flesh with his

beak, forcing out words as he said, "Your slippery snake-hood is over."

"You can't kill me," Apep hissed. "I'm a god."

"There are no gods, only evil men who prey on those ruled by fear." Willy rasped before putting an end to the evil mayor.

EPILOGUE
FOUR YEARS LATER

"Mommy, that's Daddy's statue."

"Yes, it is, Millie. That's your brave father who saved the town, and tonight, the whole town celebrates him with a midnight costume parade." Boo balanced the three-year-old toddler on her hip, rocking gently to the sound of the cover band playing "Don't Stop Believing" in the park across from city hall.

The song reminded her of Willy's faith as much as the bronze statue she stood in front of, which depicted Willy as a winged hero.

Rumors of a giant falcon appearing added to the town's folklore seemed appropriate.

The statue also represented Willy's continued heroism and bravery as an international FUC agent, after he'd protected the town from the mad mayor, faux gas leak, and resulting explosion that occurred due to the sinkhole under the cemetery.

Boo's heart had fully healed, even as she waited patiently for Willy to join her and Millie, as he'd promised to return from his latest mission.

"I want to see Grandma and Daddy," Millie said.

"Soon, very soon," Boo promised.

Millie was born with Boo's petite physical features, her skin tones a shade lighter than Boo's, along with Boo's sass and passion for adventure. She inherited her dad's focused demeanor, mocha eyes, and the tiny crook in her pinky finger.

"Boo! Millie!" Cecilia propped open the doors to the museum for the evening celebration.

Cecilia and Boo were some of the few who knew the truth of that awful night four years ago, and the disappearance of Mayor Joystick, suspected of covering up a critical soil erosion problem under the town.

The townsfolk flooded the streets in an assortment of anything-goes summer-solstice costumes, their cheers reaching the heavens as they gathered, waiting for the new mayor to kick off the summer solstice party.

"I hope you know what a hero you are, my love," Boo whispered to the statue, her pulse trilling with anticipation of Willy's arrival.

She turned her attention to Millie, who'd decided to wear falcon wings on her kitty costume. "Are you ready for the party?"

Millie wiggled free, spotting her grandmother. "Can Grandma come with us?"

The little girl didn't wait for an answer, darting across the sidewalk and springing into Cecilia's arms.

Where had time gone? Millie was thinking and making decisions, challenging Boo at every turn, it seemed.

Cecilia had become the best grandmother to Millie. Boo attributed her renewed love of her mother to Cecilia's sacrifice in slowing down Richard's attempt to take control of the Bastet statue and its fabricated power.

Without Willy's quick action, the sinkhole might have swallowed her mother right along with the mayor.

Boo shook her head, took one last look at the statue, and made her way toward the stand where the crowd gathered.

Holding hands, Millie and Cecilia met Boo.

"Let me fix you a little." Cecilia adjusted Boo's Marty McFly jacket, which had wrinkled holding Millie.

It was strange how Boo romanticized time travel movies, and that hadn't changed, even though a scientific reason existed behind the graveyard episode.

"I'm fine, Mom. Life is full of wrinkles." Boo stood firm. "I don't want to come off as perfect when I'm a work in progress."

"We all are," Cecilia conceded, adjusting her own cat ears. "Now, it's time. We'll be fine. I promise I'll keep my eyes glued to Millie during the speech."

This mothering thing wasn't as easy as she'd assumed, her worrying over Millie taking up much of her time when Willy was off saving the furry kind.

But he'd be home soon. She could feel his closeness in her bones.

With Mayor Joystick gone, she should have been calmer, but Boo knew evil existed in the world and had once made its way to Willow Wisp.

"Gosh, I'm turning into you, Mom, helicoptering the child," Boo admitted. "But I'll deal with the repercussions of her angsty teenage years later."

"I'll be there to help. Promise. Until then, let's partake in the celebration. We have a midnight parade and street lighting, line dancing..." Cecilia went on and on and kicked up her heels in a playful dance.

Millie twirled, her dress sailing about her chubby knees. "Grandma, dance with me."

The two skipped toward the gathering crowd, hand in hand.

Millie hadn't yet shifted. Boo couldn't know what her DNA would bring forth—a feline of sorts, a gorilla, or a combination shifter—but Millie was healthy and happy. For now, that was what mattered. Boo had the fierceness of motherhood to see her through helping Millie once she matured and a partner she could count on to return home.

"I can't wait to hear the mayor's speech this year."

Alyce?

A tap on Boo's shoulder spun her around. "You're here."

"I wouldn't miss the town's newest tradition. You and Willy hold a special place in my heart." The llama shifter patted the place over her breast and then hugged Boo.

Murmurs bubbled all around them as more townsfolk gathered in the hub of town, waiting for the mayor to address them.

"It's time." Boo's assistant, Ginnie, pointed to the podium.

"Go get 'em, Mayor Tagger." Alyce cheered, adding a fist pump.

Boo never thought she'd become mayor but had been unanimously voted in after the board's acting mayor, Cecilia, stepped down.

Her dream of proving herself as a worthy FUC agent had subsided after becoming a mother, and she wore her motherhood duty as a badge of honor.

Boo climbed the three steps to the raised platform and took her place behind the podium.

Familiar faces lined the street as far as she could see, and her heart warmed. Even though Willy wasn't among the crowd, yet he understood the importance of uniting the citizens in remembrance of the night the aurora borealis came to town.

Boo tapped the mic, sending a screech into the air, and the band stopped playing. "Hello. I'm Mayor Tagger, and I welcome all of you to the third annual celebration of our town heroes, especially Willy Tagger. Without your bravery, none of us would be standing here today."

Cheers erupted.

Boo's love and pride for her husband filled her to bursting. "Without further ado, let's get this party started!"

Boo blew the party horn Ginnie had left on the podium and then rejoined Cecilia and Millie. "I just need a minute."

"We'll be fine. You take your time while we watch the jugglers and pony parade." Cecilia hiked Millie onto her hip and headed to join the other parade spectators.

Maybe Boo should join in the celebration with her constituents.

She should pour her attention into her daughter in Willy's absence.

But for one night a year, from midnight until she was confident the portal wasn't reopening, she listened to the distant celebration, waiting for Willy to appear.

The grass chilled her legs as she sat near the now-closed sinkhole at her father's gravesite. The full moon filtered through the heart-shaped linden leaves and projected the pattern onto the ground, and Boo settled. She glanced upward, speaking to the moon, hoping that her dad was looking down from the heavens. "I miss you, Dad. I love you. I wish you could see your granddaughter. She's so much like you, curious, yet focused, and she's only three."

A tear fell onto Boo's cheek. She guessed the cemetery

was the appropriate place to let tears fall, and she shed less each year.

A bird cried out above, its large wings temporarily blocking the light.

Boo continued, "Dad, I will never forget you."

A thud landed behind her, and she spun to face the giant falcon.

Willy transformed into his human form. "I won't let you forget him, either. Your father saved the town by alerting to the cavernous space and tunnels running under Willow Wisp."

Excitement rushed through her, and she sprang toward Willy, clutching his neck, pulling him down for a kiss that lasted until she needed to breathe. "After three months, you're home!"

"I'll never break my promise to return to you, Boo." He took her face between his palms and lowered his mouth, crashing it against her, devouring her as if she fed his soul.

The kiss lit her inside. Over the past years, Willy had patched up every broken crack in her heart.

She took another breath and said, "You're everything to me. I'm so glad you're home..."

Boo spoke a mile a minute, but she didn't care. Willy was home. Home!

Home.

Never had one word brought her so much comfort.

He ran a slow hand down her arms as if testing her authenticity. "You're the best part of me. I love you, Boo."

That was all she needed to hear. "I love you, too."

"I have a surprise for you." Will waved at someone in the distance and then wrapped an arm around Boo's shoulders, pulling her close and providing support and comfort as the man approached.

Boo's heart marched double-time. *Dad?*

"Boo, this is your father. He remembers waking up in the hospital years ago. He had no ID on him, no memory of who he was or where he came from, but I was able to search a missing persons' database and find him using your DNA."

Her dad had returned. She didn't know any more than that he presented himself with the kindest eyes and a gentle disposition. She trusted Willy wholeheartedly.

"Boo Boo, you're all grown up." Her dad's eyes watered. "I remembered I had a daughter named Boo in the hospital."

Of course that wasn't Boo's birth name. She'd been born Emma, so a search wouldn't have led her father home.

Boo wasn't a little girl anymore, but the little girl in her caused her to run. Yes, she skipped and laughed and flew into her father's open arms. She cried from relief, and all her pain vanished. "Daddy, you're home. You're really home."

"Boo, is it really you?" He squeezed.

"It's me, Dad."

Faith had come through.

"Boo! Thom!" Cecilia called out, her mom sprinting toward them with Millie on her hip and the toddler giggling all the way.

Boo eased away and took Millie from Cecilia, handing the toddler to Willy, who embraced his daughter.

"Thom, is that really you?" Cecilia squinted.

Dad didn't waste a second. He grabbed Cecilia and spun her around. "I remember something... The night I left I met with Richard Joystick."

"You don't have to worry about him ever again," Cecilia purred.

"I'm sorry I left you, Cecilia," Thom said. "I never will again, if you'll have me."

"Will I!" Cecilia tossed her cat ears and purred as she snuggled her husband.

Boo had never seen her mom so happy, and it warmed her to her core. She had her family back—a miracle in the monsters-and-mayhem world.

She didn't know if she'd remain mayor of Willow Wisp. Willy would continue to seek adventures as a FUC agent. If so, she might join him since they'd both graduated from FUCN'A.

Their world was a blank canvas, and she was ready to paint their future.

Whatever life threw at them, she knew the truth, in her heart and soul, that they'd never be apart because they were bound by love.

"I want pizza with Grandma and Grandpa, Mommy."

Boo laughed, and the others joined in and then headed toward the festivities, leaving Willy and Boo to bask in the moonlight.

"What should we do now?" Boo asked, nuzzling the love of her life.

Willy hummed, pumping his brows. "We could celebrate our reunion, dream of our future, profess our love to each other, or... you could agree to marry me again."

"Every day," she cooed.

Willy pulled a ring from his pocket, the lapis lazuli stone twice the size of what her zebra heart pendant had been.

Willy said, "I followed the coordinates that Zeb gave you on my last mission, and I discovered this stone in a local jewelry store. It symbolizes the heavens and the gods, and, to me, my boundless love for you."

Heat welled inside her, reaching a fever pitch as Willy slid the ring onto her finger.

She squealed with joy. "Now it's time for me to *show* you how much I missed you."

Willy slid a wicked smile across his face. "I'd like that very much, *kitten*."

And Boo did. She kissed him long and slowly, again and again, finally allowing their bodies to reacquaint themselves under the spill of stars from above.

Utterly and completely.

Always and forever.

The End

And there are more FUC Academy books by other authors coming soon!

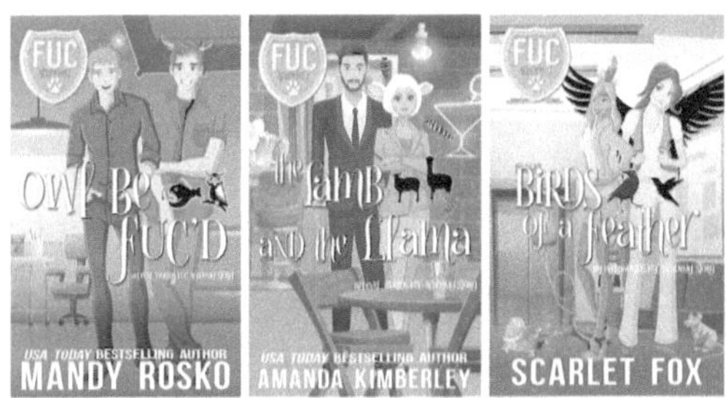

To find out more, visit worlds.EveLanglais.com or stay in the loop with our newsletter. Sign up at subscribepage.com/evelworlds

ABOUT THE AUTHOR

 *USA Today* Bestselling Author of The Faeted Vampire Series, Cyndi Faria writes steamy paranormal vampire, werewolf, & shifter romance with twist-turns you'll never see coming and happily-ever-after endings you crave. Recently, she found her passion writing zany paranormal cozies, which makes sense since her booka-holic, swearing-like-a-sailor momma taught her that silliness and shenanigans make the world a happy place.

When this California girl isn't nose-deep in a romance book, she's walking the beach, snuggling on the couch with her rescued furbabies, sipping tea, and binging on the newest paranormal release, *Vampire Diaries* reruns or her guilty pleasure, *The Bachelor*!

Website: cyndifaria.com
Newsletter Signup: dl.bookfunnel.com/h6jfaiaz77
Facebook Group Cyndi's Superstars: facebook.-com/groups/398472573898406/

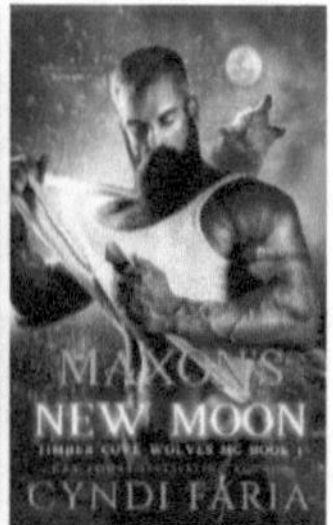

facebook.com/CyndiFariaAuthor

instagram.com/cyndifaria

tiktok.com/@authorcyndifaria

bookbub.com/authors/cyndi-faria

ALSO BY CYNDI FARIA

MONSTER AND THE JEWEL THIEF

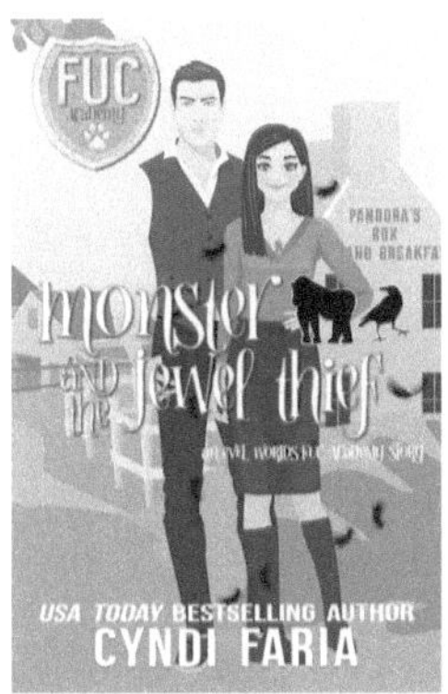

Monsters and mayhem, the FUCN'A is about to get FUC'd!

A cheese-lovin' kleptomaniac crow shifter and owner of a cozy B&B could save the day with a kick of chili flakes. That is, if Pandora Raven can escape her Lump of an ex, Monster Johnson. He's a sexy-as-a-slice-of-pepperoni-pizza-with-all-the-fixings special ops agent and has rented one of her rooms!

A four-year mission in the Amazon rainforest hunting a chimera-making mad scientist has been gorilla shifter Monster's go-to. There isn't a branch he can't swing from to nab a slippery lead. Until he learns a shocking secret back home.

Save his mate, crack the case, and, holy *pastel Azteca*, save the cheese! Oh, sweet Pandora, Monster's in her box and he's ready to make all her dreams come true.